A WINTER ANTHOLOGY

FROST

CALLIE DAHL JADE CHURCH
JENNA WEATHERWAX
HELENA V PARIS ANNIE WELCH

CONTENT WARNING

More from the authors

Callie Dahl

When Kingdoms Fall

When Balance Burns

Thieves of Starlight

Jade Church

Temper the Flame

This Never Happened

Three Kisses More

One Last Touch

Sun City series

Living in Cincy series

Ashvale series

Jenna Weatherwax

The Promise of Lightning

The Curse of Thunder

Helena V Paris

Shadows in the Deep

Ho Ho Ho bitches

FROST

THE
MOON MOTH'S
FLAME

BY CALLIE DAIIL

THE MOON MOTH'S FLAME

Dear H,

Another year has passed too quickly, bringing me and the burning flames together again for a night of misery. How I have survived ten years of this is incomprehensible. And the thought of enduring another hundred or more is positively revolting.

I often ponder over the ten-year-old me, so young and optimistic, excited to meet the girl I'd heard so much about. The girl I'd come to know and work with for the rest of my life. If I only knew then, walking into my first winter solstice celebration to meet her, what I know now.

I loathe her. She is so presumptuous—a stuck-up know-it-all.

She acts like this night revolves around her, when it is my birthday. Beyond that, it is a day to celebrate her mother and my father. We are nothing but lingering shadows, practicing for our future titles. So, I cannot fathom how unbelievably uptight she is about the minuscule performance we have performed flawlessly for a decade.

Well, almost flawlessly... Do you remember last winter's gathering? We fought because I wore the wrong kind of shoes. To make matters worse, I stepped on her toes during our dance and, in return, she pushed me hard enough to cause me to stumble back into my father's chariot. My crash into the iron wheel startled the horses, causing them to jump forward and me to fall into a hidden pile of horse manure.

I'll admit I intentionally stepped on her toes, but her reaction was much more dramatic. And if she accuses me of such tonight, I'll deny having done it on purpose, again, with every ounce of my being, just to see her get red in the face and squirm. It's the simple pleasures that bring me joy on the longest night of the year, like irritating her, and tonight will be no different. I only hope she doesn't ruin the fun for everyone again in the process.

Wish me luck and patience, the gods know I'll need it.

-M

MOTHER'S GOLDEN CHARIOT PARTED FROM THE ominous dark cloud in the east. Cheers erupted on either side of me, filling the snow-dusted canyon with victorious whistles and chants. The sun blazed brightly behind her, enhancing her golden hair and horses as she carried it through the saturated sky.

Soathag's howl thundered over the growing applause, raising the hair on my arms and neck. The eerie calls from the two sky wolves were familiar sounds, their whines, and barks often harmonizing with the morning birds and midnight owls. But every time I heard their call, my breath stilled with trepidation.

Several mortals in the crowd were standing, shouting curses to the white wolf whose barks and growls escalated the closer the blazing ball of light got. The more riled the crowd became, the further I let myself shrink into my seat, too petrified to celebrate until she was safely on the ground.

I loosened my rigid posture when Mother's horses dipped behind powdered mountain peaks that winked and glittered beneath the iridescent clouds. We had survived another day of sunlight. Releasing my clammy grip on the seat before me, I clapped while scanning the dark clouds for Soathag's figure one last time.

Tonight, we would celebrate Soathag and Hersorth's eternal attempts to hunt and swallow the sun and moon. The hunt of all hunts, for if the wolves ever caught the light carried by the gods, the world would crumble in everlasting darkness. Despite their insatiable hunger, we would dance and drink within these sacred mountains, praising the Moon and Sun God's successful seasons as they prepared for the final and most brutal season: Winter. For Hersorth, the shadowed night wolf, was vicious in his hunt, growing faster with the longer nights as if the biting cold helped aid his hunger, fueling his chase.

The Valley of the Gods always held an air of wonder, but with the day's earlier snowfall, it was positively enchanting. Dense rows of pine donned cloaks of hoarfrost creating a mirage of virescent ocean waves with crystaline foam. The field before us, which played host to various species of wildflowers and forest creatures in the summer months, was covered in a thin layer of ice and snowflakes. The snow upon it was undisturbed by the encapsulating forest, as if the creatures of winter knew what would soon take place. I wondered if they, too, took time to witness the winter solstice celebrations within the bark and frosty brambles.

Mother's golden chariot landed before us, kicking up fresh snow and dirt as it rolled to a stop. I stood with Helan, my closest friend, to better see her step from the embellished wagon. Helan looked as relieved as I felt. Her mother was a renowned goddess as mine was, so she knew what it was like to fear for our parents every day, wondering and hoping we wouldn't have to take over their positions before we were ready. I shuddered to think of Helan taking over her mother's position while breezing over her long silver hair and beady midnight eyes to focus on my mother.

I was envious of Mother's opulent stature and wondered if I would ever reach her level of regal elegance. Her strappy silk dress seemed to be made of melting gold, the train of it followed her graceful steps like a slow cascading waterfall. Her windblown hair settled in sandy waves above her lower back, practically glowing atop her bronzed skin, and a tiara made of shimmering copper spikes protruded high above her brows like bolts of lightning. She was born to greet the crowds, shining brighter than the sun as she did, while I shook harder than an autumn leaf if I had to speak to a gathering of even three people.

It was one of two reasons why our winter solstice celebration was my least favorite, knowing I'd soon have to leave the safety of the crowd to join her below. Thankfully, I didn't have to speak in front of the gathered gods and mortals... but I was required to perform.

A dance. One song. Three minutes in length.

For such a short moment in time, its fleeting harmony was something that vexed me time and time again. I practiced every night in the comfort of my bedroom's balcony, hoping to look half as fluid and delicate as my mother did, to no avail. How was I supposed to one day step into my mother's place if I couldn't even master the steps to a three-minute dance? How was I supposed to carry the sun when I spent my days cowering in its shadow?

As Mother helped hand out bubbling wine to the crowd, I shifted from side to side, nervously humming to the band's spirited tune until I felt *him*.

The second reason for my disfavor of the winter solstice was because of the Moon God's son, Motti. Someone I had been intrinsically paired with since the day I was born, he was my polar opposite in looks and attitude, though, in work, we would be equals and would have to work together seamlessly to keep the wolves at bay. He was the god I would work with for the rest of my life once we took our parent's position.

If only the mortals and other gods knew how badly we hated one another. It wasn't always like this. At first, I enjoyed his presence and would have even gone as far as to say I had a small, girlish attraction to him. That was until he became positively infuriating.

"Nervous, Sunbeam?" The flesh on my bare back rose from the too-familiar feeling of his icy gaze. Despite my lingering disdain for the arrogant god, our cosmic link to one another set my nerves on fire whenever he neared.

Yes. "Of course not." I straightened my posture, ignoring his black-clad figure sauntering up beside me. "You smell much better than last year."

"A memory I'm sure you'll never forget."

My nostrils flared with amusement while Helan coughed to cover her abrupt giggle. I allowed myself a quick glance, noting the tick in Motti's jaw. My smile bloomed from his annoyance.

The memory of him falling in horse manure would forever be one of my favorites to call on whenever I needed a pick-me-up. It was almost better than the memory of me shoving him into the drink table when we were fourteen after he'd poked fun at the bright and awkward skin blemishes on my forehead and nose—something even growing gods and goddesses had to deal with as they matured.

Motti leaned forward to inspect Helan and her dramatic black gown. "Looking deathly as ever, little reaper."

She scoffed in reply and turned to leave, only to be stopped by my tight hold on her wrist.

Helan ignored my silent plea and gave us both a callous look. "You two may be forced to endure one another's company, but I am not." Her beady eyes met mine, and she winked before vanishing.

I blinked in awe at the sudden empty space where she once stood, envying her ability to disappear whenever she pleased.

Motti frowned at where she'd been and grumbled, "I forget manners hardly matter when you live with the dead."

His cerulean eyes trailed down my dress towards my covered shoes. Motti gave a criticizing hum while cocking his head to inspect the sewn details of my gown better.

My temper flared, forcing me to face him fully. "What?"

Motti shrugged and lifted his drink. A smirk was forming behind his raised glass, half covering his mouth while the cup's brim rested on his lips. "I simply find you very brave choosing such a long, layered skirt this year. It would be a shame to trip under such a heavy garment." He took a long pull from the glass and sighed. "But with all the practicing you've been doing, perhaps you'll be just fine."

My body stiffened. What would Motti know about my practice? The thought of him knowing how hard both this dance and my nerves were to master sent my pulse racing. I shouldn't be ashamed, but I knew he'd hold it over my head somehow, for it was another way to show how easy everything was for him.

"I'll be fine if you don't sabotage this night for me. *Again.*"

"Are you accusing me of something, Brenna?" The way he said my name held an arrogant challenge, igniting my temper further.

"Of course I am. You stepped on me!" I countered icily. "I could barely walk for a week after! Half of my foot was bruised. That was no accident, Motti, admit it."

Motti bridged the little gap between us. Our bitter tension snapped into my rising pulse with his sudden movement. His black velvet jacket rubbed against my crossed arms, sending an unwarranted shiver through me.

From lowered lids, he shot me a dark look. "And was pushing me into horse manure an accident?"

I had to lift my chin slightly to meet his gaze, noting how tall he had grown since the summer solstice. "Yes."

"I assume that makes us even."

"Perhaps."

Frigid fingers grazed my arm, making me flinch, and I looked down to find Motti's open palm resting on my crossed arms.

My brows furrowed while he spoke, "Let's start this year with a clean slate. We're too old for games."

I hesitated for a moment, wondering what sort of joke he was playing. When he didn't continue, the look in his eyes surprisingly serious, I wondered if he truly had matured this year.

"Swear on it," I said, ignoring the bitter taste of apprehension on my tongue.

"I swear."

Our palms met, sending another jolting tremor through me.

After ten years, one would think I would not react to Motti's touch—but I did every time, without fail. His skin seemed to be made from the frost blanketing the forest around us, while mine was stitched together by the last few threads of summer.

Warning bells rang within me, urging me to release our

firm grasp on one another, but I stilled when a snowflake landed on his thumb. Another landed on my knuckles, and it melted before I could study its intricate design upon my bronze complexion. My nose scrunched as a small puff of steam arose from where the snowflake had once been.

A pang of jealousy rippled through our touch. I couldn't help but wonder what it was like to preserve such intricate moments, like the details of snowflakes, so effortlessly. He was created for the night—a place where such fleeting moments were held tightly. Moments that would melt beneath the sun's remorseless rush.

"You can let go of me now, Sunbeam."

"And you can stop calling me that," I snapped, ignoring the warmth that crawled up my neck to settle on my cheeks. "We're not thirteen."

I yanked my hand from him, noting the soft brush of his thumb along my knuckles while I slipped from his grasp. I stilled from the gentle gesture, but Motti was already turning away from me, his gaze cold and distant.

My stomach tightened when I caught him wiping his thumb and palm vigorously with a cloth as if our touch disgusted him so fervently. I shook my head, chastising myself for thinking that slight movement was a glimmer of something other than hatred between the two of us. But maybe this truce would end our petty pranks and loathing, creating room for friendship as we had at the beginning of meeting each other. Or, at the very least, respect.

Motti's father, Ilo, was breaking through the treelines, causing icicles to fall and shatter from the branches he swiftly disturbed. His white hair was a stark contrast to the dark embellishments around him. Two brilliant silver horses led his iron chariot towards Mother's. The crowd was frantic once more, eager for the Sun and Moon's Waltz to begin.

The sky was fading from dusk's soft pinks and purples to a deepening blue around us. Motti's midnight navy hair was beginning to shimmer in response, tiny specks of starlight appearing through his still-damp strands. I hated how polished he looked despite arriving late, as he did every year, almost as much as I hated his perfectly crooked nose and high-cut cheekbones. His pale skin began to glow, matching the moon's gentle light, enhancing his ethereal nature and it took everything in me not to call him a glowworm. I checked my hair, drawn to cascade over the left side of my neck, noting the pink and purple hues darkening with the sky. Motti and I were the blooming moments before the sun and moon's rise, forever dancing in the other's shadow.

I pushed out a nervous breath while running a hand over my gown. The fabric was simple enough. A silk-covered corset with sheer, pink bell sleeves ending at my elbows. The skirt was layered in three rounds of silk and orange chiffon, creating an easy yet effective illusion of a flame trailing behind me while I walked or spun in circles. I wouldn't let Motti get to me. I had practiced in this dress for weeks and had only tripped on the bottom of the skirt twice. I would be fine.

Hersorth's howl rolled towards us from the west, the sound long and haunting. The wolf's yearning tone stirred my nerves, and a sudden wave of nausea rolled into my throat. I held my stomach with a concerned grimace.

Motti didn't so much as flinch or check the skies as the night wolf's howl grew louder, as if he held no worry that the large black wolf would hunt him one day. I wish I had his calm resolve, despite how often it vexed me, especially now as my stomach rolled again in time with the wolf's cry.

"My friend and I had a bet," Motti drawled while watching his father wave to the crowd.

"On?"

"How long would you wait to bring up what I did last year. I thought you would wait to accuse me of stepping on you until we started dancing. He guessed it would be the first thing you brought up. Seems he was right."

My head cocked as I asked carefully, "And what did he win?"

Hersorth howled again and Motti's eyes flicked to the clouds above before meeting mine.

"I've realized after all our years of friendship that he deals in pride and bragging rights. His prize will be the joy of once again besting me." His eyes glittered. "Perhaps I'll come out of this evening with the upper hand. The night is still young, Sunbeam."

"We made a truce, Motti," I warned.

Motti only laughed, finishing his drink with shaking shoulders before disappearing into the crowd. I grumbled and trailed after him, sending a silent prayer to the gods that Motti would stick to his word, and I wouldn't puke in front of the hundreds gathered around me.

H,

She puked during the dance.

All over my suit. And then some more on the ground between us.

How was I supposed to know the market balm I'd confiscated would cause her body to react so violently? Countless hours of research had me believing it would only give her a fever, hot flashes, and, at the very worst, a slight rash for only a few hours.

I had hoped she would call off the dance for feeling ill, but I forgot how stubborn the sun brat is, and I had to wear that reminder on me for the rest of the evening while she was sent home to rest before the feast even began.

To make matters worse, I left the concoction on my palm for too long as it sunk into her skin during our handshake.

She had distracted me, taking in the touch of our hands with puzzling scrutiny. I have never seen her look at me in such a way, as if I were someone she didn't hate. As if I suddenly had something to offer her. But of course I don't. She was probably just plotting my demise.

And now I write this, drowning in a pool of sweat, miserable from my stomach's cramping.

It pains me to admit, dear friend, that

our foul little sun goddess looked radiant tonight. She has always been beautiful in her offbeat, wild way, as most flames are. The type of beauty you fear to touch or stand near, for it is all-consuming. A dangerous thought that has led men to war time and time again.

Beauty blinds and binds, hiding the wolf beneath the glamour. It was almost enough to make me feel remorse for how catastrophic this plan was.

I'll admit, I am terrified of her retaliation. Perhaps it's wise to begin preparing for next winter solstice. Let me know if you have any ideas but please, no herbs, balms, or tonics.

-M

H,

I should be out celebrating my twenty-first birthday, but I cannot help but feel melancholy after tonight's event.

There was no dance, at least not with the sun goddess and I.

Her mother announced we would not dance because Brenna had hurt her leg the day before in the stables. At first, I didn't believe the story until I caught the limping bob of her sunset hair within the crowd.

I couldn't even defend myself from whatever prank I thought the sun brat would have ready for me, for there was none. She avoided me all evening, watching where I stood so she could remain half a field away at all times.

Don't mock me, as I'm sure you are while reading this part. I didn't watch her the whole evening, as it sounds above. It's not my fault that her light so furiously bobs brighter than the rest. I kept catching myself following where she had been, but I was always too far behind to feel the lashing heat of her anger. Something I never thought I would miss. Yet I sit, looking out of my balcony facing hers, feeling... regret.

Will I apologize for last winter? Never. But I do have an odd ache in my chest. One that makes me ponder how our next run-in will go.

Ps.

Now that I think of it, the infuriating girl was outside last night practicing our dance on her balcony, as she always does.

It seems I was pranked all along, for she faked it all to avoid me.

What a clever, infuriating goddess.

Perhaps I'll fake my death next year and retire from all of this before it even begins. I'd love to see the shock on her face if I did.

-M

H,

I drank too much — or not enough, for I wish I could have woken up without the memory of what we did. Instead, I awoke today thinking only of her and haven't stopped since.

Everyone was dancing around the bonfire to celebrate the summer solstice when she appeared before me. I readied myself for her revenge from two winters before, but it never came.

She had been crying. Her eyes were red-rimmed, and her cheeks were flushed like they get when she is angry. I knew why. Everyone at the gathering did. She and her dismal boyfriend had gotten into a rather public argument and when it escalated, he stormed out.

He left her on the night of her birthday! How pathetic. The solstices are our only nights of reprieve from the ever-constant fear of the wolves. How does he not understand? Even I, who loathes the sun brat more than anyone, would never stoop so low. Even if we fought, I wouldn't leave.

Perhaps that's why she found me in the crowd. Understanding I was the only person to feel the way she did, despite our history.

I was startled when she pulled me in to dance with her, but I didn't stop her. I couldn't pull away, too ensnared by the heat of her touch and the rash fever in her glassy eyes.

This was different from our winter dance. This was free of frozen, rigid structure. It was warm, frenzied, and all-consuming. I was both the tree bark burning within the fire and the flames devouring it all at once. And

I was out of body, as if in a fever dream, until her lips crashed into mine. The kiss had me tumbling back into my frame to see the horror on her face, while I struggled to remember what my life was like before giving into her flames.

The petty pranks and games are over.

She's won, and nothing will ever be the same again.

-M

H,

We have written to each other daily for a decade, and now you choose to stop contact? When I need my friend the most, you disappear.

You may not ever read this, and I no longer care. I just need someone to carry this weight, even if it's only the paper holding the ink that solidifies my thoughts.

Tonight, I take Father's place. I thought I had been friends with fear before, but I had no idea I'd only been its acquaintance.

It's taken me two days to understand

that he is truly gone. Two nights of darkness to understand Hersorth attacked him instead of taking the moon. Why? Because he knew I was not ready for this? Was he bored of the struggle to chase Father and hoped our race would be more satisfactory?

I am not ready for this. I never was.

-M

THE DEATH OF THE MOON GOD HAD SENT A shockwave through the realm. The winter storm to follow was relentless, hovering over the winter solstice celebration like a blanket of grief.

We knew the night wolf, Hersorth, was cold and calculating, but no one could have predicted his attack on Ilo. Motti was his only son. We should have had eight years to each find love and make a family to continue our lineage before taking our parents' positions. If Hersorth knew this, he was changing his centuries-old hunt to stop the cycle of new, fresh gods. And if he caught Motti, no one could keep the moon from him.

Motti had stepped into his new role as gracefully as he could, but the death of Ilo had unleashed a new level of power from Hersorth.

It wasn't just the night wolf—- Soathag's chase for the sun had become ravenous. Mother was struggling each day, as were her horses. Though she persisted, her light was dimming, making me wonder if a part of her soul passed when Ilo did. She would always love my father, who had died when I was just a baby, but she and Ilo had an undeniable bond with their shared celestial titles. It had been two months since his passing, and each night, I found her wandering the halls like a lost spirit, looking out of the windows toward the moon. If Soathag didn't catch her, the weight of her mourning and exhaustion would.

It was a wonder we were celebrating with the state of the realm and Mother and Motti's shared exhaustion, but the mortals needed to see us tonight. We needed to show them that we would endure.

My stomach turned when Motti emerged from the frosted treeline. His smile beamed with confidence as he raced towards the crowd in the iron chariot.

I admired Motti for how collected he remained, given the circumstances. Meanwhile, I selfishly woke up each morning ready to vomit. Despite her fatigue, Mother was teaching me more every night, as if she were preparing for the worst. I knew I wasn't ready for this. Even with my thousands of lessons, I worried if I ever really would be.

I wove through the people as Motti rolled his chariot up to Mother's, stopping beside her. The two exchanged words while she pulled him in for a half hug. A wave of sorrow rolled through me as Mother wiped at her eyes hastily while clinging to Motti. But she gathered herself quickly and turned her horses to wave and smile to those who called her name.

This close, I could see the cracks around the Moon God's carefree mask. A mask I never cared to study until the summer solstice when I foolishly kissed him. I don't know why I had sought him out after two years of avoiding him. I was drunk or heartbroken—maybe both. I didn't even realize he was what I was searching for until my feet stopped right before his. It was as if our souls were bound by the same thread, constantly tugging and pulling on one another's last nerves.

The flames upon his face had cast him in a different light as I watched him dance and laugh with a sad smile, knowing the saccharine sound would die the second he spotted me. I couldn't remember how we had gotten to the point of hating one another so badly and I couldn't find a reason to continue do so as I saw a glimpse of the Motti from our youth. Desperate to keep that version of him, I danced with him, giving into the freeing rhythm of my fire and his frost. And gods, it was better than any carefully mapped-out, polished act. I had never felt so normal. There was no fear of wolves as we danced. There was no sadness or anger. It was just me and the Moon, orbiting one another while the rest of the world quieted.

But then I kissed him.

Balance was needed between the Moon and Sun, and that kiss had melted the scales. The touch was euphoric and addictive, but as consuming as it felt, the wave of panic that crashed into me next had me running for my life.

I was grateful for our time apart so I could find a way to convince myself that lust and loathing should not coexist. But now, as he walked toward me, the two lines blended beneath his calculated steps.

The constellations in Motti's navy blue hair had washed away with Ilo's passing. His new snow-colored strands fit his bitter attitude, making him look more like his father than ever before. The curls that had once hovered above his shoulders were nowhere to be found, and the little length he had left uncut was tucked behind his ears. He bore a formal, silver cape attached to a royal blue jacket and it flowed behind him, creating a snow flurry to kick up beneath his steps. He had always been infuriatingly handsome, but tonight he was magnificent.

I frowned and looked down at my attire. My navy velvet gown matched Motti's suit, as if they were made by the same seamstress. Even my silver gloves coordinated perfectly with his dramatic cape.

As the Moon God sauntered my way, I braced myself for some snide remark, but I found myself stunned in silence as he breezed past me without so much as a glance.

Grumbling in irritation, I trailed after him. I had to lift my skirts to keep up, and when he continued to ignore me, I reached out my hand to stop him.

Motti wheeled around, focusing his glare on my embrace. His chest heaved up and down as if my touch was hurting him. I pulled my hand away as quickly as I could, but he continued to focus on where it had been with a deepening scowl.

Dark purple circles hung beneath Motti's eyes and his cheeks were more profound than usual. His carefree mask wasn't cracking, it was hanging on by a fragile thread.

"When was the last time you slept, Motti?"

The way he scrutinized me was venomous as he sneered. "I'm in no mood for your games tonight, Brenna."

"I'm not playing games." With an exasperated sigh, I explained, "I'm making sure you're okay."

"I understand I went too far with our pranks two years ago. For that, I am regretful. I will apologize if that is what it takes to make you stop!"

I shook my head, brows furrowing. "Stop what?"

"Stop pretending to care. Stop torturing me." His pale cheeks were red with anger as he waited for a response, focusing on my lips with open disdain.

Oh. My hands clasped together, and I gnawed on my

bottom lip while searching for the proper wording. His focus narrowed on the movement, making me flush and stop instantly. "I'm sorry for what I did that summer solstice. It was a mistake. But I feel like that hardly matters with what has happened since."

He cocked his head slowly, evaluating my words with frigid precision.

I continued in a rush, as if worried he was a rabbit ready to turn and bolt. "I'm trying to be your friend. What happened to Ilo was terrible, and you don't need to carry that burden alone." My eyes watered as I remembered Ilo helping us when Father passed. Sometimes, he helped with meals or duties, but most memories were of him simply existing in our space. Filling the void to help ease the weight of grief. I failed to hide the thick emotion as I said softly, "Let me help you. Like Mother and Ilo helped each other."

"We owe each other nothing."

My jaw hung slack as if his words had slapped me. Ice spread through my stomach and crawled into my lungs, tightening my throat. My pulse drummed in my ears, quieting the shock of his words, only to make way for the subtle sting of disappointment.

"Right." I looked down at the snow to hide the flush upon my cheeks. "Of course. You're right."

The punching sound of crunching snow broke our rising tension. Motti focused his glare on the movement behind me, and I flinched when a warm hand grazed my lower back.

"There you are!" Hálkon's honeyed voice warmed the previous chill from Motti's words.

Hálkon's olive cheeks and nose were red from the cold, showing how perfectly mortal he was. His black hair was slicked back behind his ears, and his amber eyes practically glowed while he smiled at me. He was handsome in a simple way and, above all, kind. He worked up in our mountains during the spring and summer, helping with our land and horses. We had grown up together while sharing the same unspoken attraction, and it wasn't until he approached me shortly after the summer solstice that I knew he felt our odd connection, too. In some ways, he reminded me of my father, with his contemplative conversations and patient nature. The opposite of the one sending daggers into my still-heated cheeks.

Hálkon must have felt the tension he'd so casually walked into. How could he not? It nearly choked me as Motti hovered before us, his dark energy brewing like a lightning-filled storm cloud. Hálkon glanced at Motti and me with a questioning brow but said nothing. Instead, he handed me a steaming mug, reminding me he had gone to get us drinks before Motti's arrival.

I murmured thanks, taking a careful sip, hoping the warm apple cider would wash away the awkwardness. Hálkon took a sip as well, giving me another questioning look.

My throat cleared, and I realized how rude I was. "Motti, this is H-"

Motti abruptly cut me off. "Hálkon, yes. I know."

Hálkon extended his hand, and Motti quickly shook it, his jaw ticking. My mouth opened and closed as I struggled to find a way to ask how they knew each other.

Motti shifted rigidly, returning his hand to tuck it into his jacket pocket. "He works for us too, Sunbeam," he drawled.

I narrowed my eyes at the sudden arrival of the nickname. Hálkon looked down at his shoes before taking a sip of his drink, and I took a protective step towards him.

"And when did this little union happen?" Motti asked, waving a finger between Hálkon and me.

"Shortly after the summer solstice." I muttered uneasily. Composure was a fragile shell around me as I struggled to avoid the memory of Motti's lips on mine.

Motti's mouth parted in surprise while Hálkon's smile bloomed from my words.

Hálkon cut through the building pressure, speaking with ease. "I've been rather excited to attend tonight. The lower realms buzz frequently about the dances."

The Moon God narrowed his eyes on Hálkon as if he were prey. "Is that so? And is there a favorite among mortals?" The pompous way he said *mortals* made me want to throw my hot cider on him.

Hálkon's smile widened. If he was aware of Motti's passive jests, he was determined not to show it. I felt myself melting into his side, enamored over his patience as he spoke. "Yours. They say your dance is like fire and water chasing one another, much like the wolves' endless hunt." He brought his hand back to wrap around my waist, pulling me in so we were flush. "Brenna doesn't like to talk about it, so I was eager to travel tonight to witness it myself."

"It's nothing special," I murmured.

"Always so modest." Hálkon kissed my temple, and I stiffened. "I am beyond fortunate to see you dance tonight," he said sweetly into my braided hair.

A thick wave of resentment barreled into me from Motti's towering frame and I chastised myself for looking at him to avoid Hálkon's sudden heat.

Motti's eyes were dancing between the two of us, his eyes sparkling maliciously. This wouldn't end well. Motti was in a foul mood, desperate to throw it on someone else, and I would not allow Hálkon to be the victim of his anger.

"We should go," I said to Motti with a hint of warning. His lips folded into a sneer, but he reached for my hand without further comment.

"I'll see you after," Hálkon said warmly, and I nodded before giving him a quick peck on the lips.

Before Hálkon could deepen the kiss, Motti's fingers curled tightly around mine and he pulled me from Hálkon's embrace.

I gave an apologetic smile to Hálkon over my shoulder and he returned it with pinched brows, his eyes darting between Motti and me.

Motti said nothing, his cold anger plummeting into dangerous temperatures with every step we took. I was beginning to feel whiplash from his words while being drowned in the undercurrent of his rage. Was this not what he wanted? He asked for no games, and I proved I was not playing any by bringing Hálkon to the dance. He should have felt relief that I wasn't determined to be his demise, only to truly be his friend. Even if I had thought of kissing Motti several times since the summer solstice, it didn't mean I would ever do it again. I had witnessed what feelings like this could do to others. I saw it now as Mother withered away. It couldn't happen again. I wouldn't let it.

So why did I feel guilty for kissing Hálkon in front of Motti?

Desperate to squash the growing rift between us, I rolled my shoulders and spoke with determination. "We owe each other nothing, remember?"

"Right," Motti huffed coldly. He straightened and dropped my hand to step away as we neared the center of the snow-blanketed valley.

A drum began to beat in slow, steady pulses. The sound drilled into the soles of my shoes and racing pulse.

Motti and I circled one another, matching the drum's rhythm. On our third rotation, we tightened our steps, and the drum's pace quickened. We regarded one another as I raised my hands above my head. He mirrored my actions, stepping towards me as if to bring his palms to mine, but then we both pushed away from the invisible wall between us, held up by our earlier tension.

We spun towards the crowd and then back to each other and I lowered one hand to rest on my hip while the other extended toward Motti. His fingers gripped my wrist as he pulled me into his chest.

His voice was bitter in my ear, causing me to fumble over my inward count. "You said you wanted to help me earlier. That you are not playing games."

"I did," I said breathlessly, trying to catch up on our count.

"If you really want to help, then start by admitting that what happened on summer solstice was far from a mistake. That the mortal boy you brought is a distraction from whatever this is."

Shock rippled through me as I spun from his grasp, just in time for the tempo shift. The music was deafening, the band's instruments hauntingly crisp as the crowd clapped and pounded their feet into the snow in time to match the drums.

Anger fueled by Motti's words ate away my usual nerves as I ran toward him. I pushed off the ground, my heels slipping in the snow, and leaped. Before I could fall, he caught me as gracefully as he always did, lifting my chest over his head. I rested my hands on his shoulders, squeezing tighter than necessary, and I felt his fingers dig into my hips in response. I smiled at the crowd before glaring at him.

Motti lowered me slowly in time with the music. Every year, we avoided looking at one another during this part. It was too intimate for us, our faces borderline touching while he slowly set me back in the snow. Tonight, I didn't care. I wanted him to see how much I loathed him. I wanted him to feel my anger as our noses touched. I needed to prove the lust I felt from the summer kiss was only a ruse. But as his breath tickled my lips, my stomach flipped with my rising pulse as if to argue with my stubborn notions.

Back on the ground, I turned to lean on his chest. His fingers tapped along my hip with the beat, eliciting rows of goosebumps beneath my gown. He always did that, reminding me of the song's count, as if to assume I had forgotten.

We swayed together, the easy movement returning me to the summer solstice when we melted into one another, dancing as one body.

Motti's voice crawled over me as he asked, "Do you think this is how the wolves feel? An aching hunger of being so close to what they yearn the most?" His nose brushed over my ear, and his breath upon my neck sent a rush of fire and snow through my veins.

"I am with Hálkon," I said coldly, despite the tremor in my voice.

"For how long, Brenna? Will the two of you meet every evening after your long, hard days of running from Soathag? You know he will never understand what you go through, Sunbeam. He'll never relate to your fear of the wolves."

I turned and ran from the truth in his words as quickly

as the snow would allow. Then, right as the drums hit their loudest beat, they stopped.

I slid to a stop with the music, standing on the tips of my toes before falling backward gracefully.

Startled cries and gasps came from the crowd, as if they hadn't seen the same move for over a decade, and Motti caught me before my head hit the ground. He pushed me up, and I spun as he did, only for him to catch me again. My arms wrapped around his neck, and our foreheads touched.

Our chests heaved from the rapid movements as he spoke, "You know he cannot fill the void of unease you carry like a crown. Would he offer to carry your burden as you did for me earlier?"

"Would you?" I snarled the question.

He lifted me before answering.

I left the safety of his hands for two seconds, then three, spinning in the air with my arms tucked.

When I landed back in his arms, the crowd erupted with their usual astonishment and I smiled, relieved to have finished the dance with no mistakes. Tonight's anger had seemed to help quiet my constant overthinking.

Motti smiled proudly as if he knew our arguing had helped this be our best dance yet.

My lips curled from his arrogance. "I know you heard my question, Motti. Answer me." He avoided my glare, his jaw ticking, and I scoffed. "That's what I thought. Keep your thoughts to yourself."

Our kiss was a mistake.Wondering if he cared for me at all was a mistake. We didn't need to be friends, and we certainly didn't need to be near each other now that our dance was done.

I pushed out of his embrace with more force than

necessary, but his hands gripped my wrists to pull me in closer. I gasped as Motti dipped me to the ground.

His hands held me firmly as he spoke, "Of course I'd bear your burdens, Brenna. I'd wear them proudly, like decorated medals, to see you walk weightlessly for one night." Motti's voice was flame upon my face as his lips brushed mine. "It fuels your resentment towards me because you've always known. We felt it this summer and have been running ever since."

"Known what?" I asked, my fingers digging into his biceps to keep from falling back into the snow.

"That we are inevitable." And then he kissed me.

Motti lifted me into a stand. His hand hovered over my lower back, not daring to touch me now, as we bowed to the crowd. The sweltering anger rippling from my heaving shoulders was palpable, but the applause was louder than ever. Their reaction to the kiss fueled my rage, stoking the fire within.

My pulse was loud in my ears as I turned, focusing on the trees ahead of me. I needed to get away and think before I incinerated Motti for his careless actions.

His footsteps were quick behind me, making me walk faster. I hardly felt the branch that scraped along my cheek as I pushed into the snow-covered rows of pine.

I heard it snap against Motti, his annoyed growl giving me sick satisfaction.

"Brenna," Motti warned. I lifted my skirts to run. "Brenna!"

His grasp was firm against my wrist, but I pulled hard enough for my hand to slip out of my glove. Motti held it wide-eyed, and I didn't waste the opportunity to flee. When he reached for me again, I whirled on him.

The slap echoed between the branches—crisp and

biting, like the temperature trying desperately to cool my temper.

Motti gaped at my open palm, still hovering beside his red cheek, before glaring at me.

"I know you better than anyone, Brenna—more than that mortal. When you're scared, you run. You hide." He stalked closer. "I don't have the luxury of hiding anymore, so neither do you. We need to face whatever this is because you and I know it has been brewing for over a decade."

"There is nothing to face," I grit out. My eyes were blurred with rage-filled tears as I raised my palm to slap him again, but Motti caught my wrist.

His other hand wrapped around me as he walked me to the nearest tree. Pine needles poked into my back as Motti pushed us through the branches until I hit the trunk with a gasp.

Snow fell over us both while the rows of pine settled, cascading us in darkness. The soft moon glow of his skin was the only light, allowing me to see the frustration in his gaze as he looked down at me, bracing his hands on either side of my face to keep me from bolting.

"Do you know what our names mean?" Motti asked in a harsh, raw voice.

I glared at him, keeping quiet. I didn't want to face this. Facing it could be more dangerous than the wolves' endless hunt. Cold air greeted me when Motti pushed away from the tree's trunk. I watched, motionless, as he pulled off one leather glove and the other.

"Brenna means *the great fire when all others go out*." He dropped the gloves into the snow between us, the movements tense and rigid while he studied me.

"And yours?" I asked hoarsely, giving into curiosity.

Motti paused for a beat, lips thinning. "*Moth.*"

I couldn't stop the abrupt laugh that fell from my mouth.

Oh, the mighty Moon God, named after one of the simplest night creatures.

He smiled in response, and I stilled as his thumb brushed over my chin.

"I used to hate your laugh," Motti mused, squashing the little humor I had found. "Every year, I'd find new ways to torment you, knowing it was the only joy I'd be able to keep for myself. But when I look back to those memories, I only see sparse moments of your laugh." Brushing his hand over my bottom lip, he whispered, "Your smile. Neither directed towards me, of course, but oh, how I began to crave such things. I think it made me hate you more to know I'd never feel the warmth of the sun as others feel, for I am the one who is always left behind to burn. "

"Motti, stop."

"I won't." He shook his head. "Yes, I was selfish tonight. You have every reason to hate me for it. If this is the last time we speak, so be it. But I won't let you run until you hear how I have survived Hersorth these last two brutal months. They say names carve the path of our fate with their definition. Despite what I felt, I convinced myself our names held no merit until you kissed me on summer solstice."

The look he gave me stripped me bare. I turned my head only to be stopped by cold fingers.

Motti's voice was soft as he tugged my chin to face him. "When a moth finds a flame, everything else ceases to exist for them. It doesn't matter where they had been going or what they had been doing before they found this great light, for it is suddenly wiped from memory. The fire is the moth's new beginning and end."

His nearness overwhelmed me with his raw, unmasked words. My heart beat frantically in my chest, still desperate to run, while my body seemed to sink into the snow, rooting to the tree we leaned against.

A smile trembled over his lips as he continued to fill the silence. "After you kissed me, I realized I've sought out your light since we were ten. Even as we fought, I stayed by your side to feel the warmth of your lashing anger, for it kept me warm for months after. When Father died, the only person I wanted to see was you. Everything was so dark. And cold. I've never been so cold. No light could warm me, not when compared to yours. Every night with the moon has been focused on seeing you again. *Just one more week,* I'd tell myself as Hersorth's teeth snapped too close behind me. *Just one more night until I feel her flame once more.*"

I was surprised to find my thumb wiping the tear from his cheek as he spoke and flinched when I saw him doing the same for me, not realizing I had also been crying.

"I was selfish for kissing you tonight. I am selfish for wanting to do it again and again." My breath hitched as icy fingers laced into my braid, tilting my mouth towards his. "Tell me I'm wrong, Brenna. Tell me to find another's light, and I'll go."

"It's only lust. You'll find another flame, Moon Moth." I tried to laugh, but it caught in my throat. We couldn't do this. Ilo's death had changed Mother. Only undeniable love could do that. I couldn't cross that line with Motti. If something happened to one of us, the other wouldn't survive it. "We are not inevitable. We can't be."

My pulse rose with the lie, and I arched as Motti's grip tightened on my hair.

He smiled, whispering into my parted lips, "Prove it."

Our lips met, igniting a song within my veins. Its beat was frantic and all-consuming.

Much like our dance, when I moved, Motti countered gracefully. My hands slid onto his chest, my fingers fumbling to undo the buttons of his jacket.

His hand left my hair to cup my neck as he explored my mouth eagerly, his lips tracing mine before nipping at my chin and ear. I sucked in the crisp air as he licked my neck, softly biting my collarbone before kissing his way back up to my mouth.

Motti shrugged his way out of his jacket, speeding up my fumbling attempt to remove it. I palmed the thin cotton shirt tucked into his dress pants, then traced a finger down his chest. His forehead rested on mine and he panted, watching my finger move slowly down his abdomen. I stopped just above the buttons of his trousers, and his stomach tightened with anticipation. I teased him and moved my finger lower at a glacial pace.

A rough, tormented groan caught in Motti's throat, and he gripped my hips impatiently. I stopped teasing him to wrap my hands around his neck.

Motti lifted me eagerly and lowered his hands to cup my backside and my legs wrapped around his waist, pushing my dress up, eliciting a shiver from the biting cold. But the chill liquified as Motti pressed me against the bark.

Heat rippled into our touch, sending a tremor of anticipation through me. His lips brushed over mine as his hips ground into me and I gasped when he moved again, pressing into me, rippling a tight awareness to my core.

"Brenna." My name was like a parting plea from his lips before I kissed his mouth with savage intensity. His body trembled, and I smiled against him, knowing his restraint was shattering with every move I made.

Hersorth's familiar howl rumbled over the trees, shaking free clumps of snow and pine, and I tensed, the heat in my core freezing as the wolf howled again.

Feeling my sudden change, Motti pulled away to study my face. He lowered me, stepping away with a tormented gaze, making room for thickly barbed vines of unease and animosity to grow into a wall of thorns between us once again.

Oh gods, what had we just done? What had I just done? Hálkon was waiting for me, and here I was, wrapped around the man and god I'd sworn I'd always loathe.

I adjusted the skirts of my dress with shaking fingers, avoiding his gaze.

"Brenna." The longing in Motti's voice was the final thread to snap my resolve.

My heart was already breaking from the fear of how I felt. We needed to survive the wolves. There was no room for more uncertainty. There was no room for such hope when we could only endure.

My chest heaved as I vowed with venom, "We are not inevitable." And before I could memorize the hurt on his face, I turned and ran.

I HAD BEEN PACING IN FRONT OF THE MIRROR FOR ten minutes. Every time I caught my reflection, more golden strands appeared, wiping away the pink and purple saturation with every new hair.

Mother's grief and strain had festered into a deep-rooted sickness that appeared like a plague in the early summer. Despite her slow decline, she still managed to carry the sun. But when Soathag nearly caught her yesterday afternoon, I knew everything was about to change.

It was like being tethered to her soul while watching her finish her ride through the sky. Waves of grief and relief barreled into me as Mother tucked the sun into the mountains for the evening, and I knew then she was saying goodbye to her closest friend. I knew when I saw the first few golden strands weave through my braid as she took her time riding home with her horses. And when Helan appeared in my room an hour ago to deliver the news, I knew it was my time.

Throughout my upbringing, any mention or thought of taking Mother's position made me want to hide and vomit. But now, as I finally stopped to look at myself in the mirror, I felt a surprising sense of resolve. Soathag didn't catch her, and he never would. All I had to do was ride as fast as I could every day, and my fate could be the same. Motti had proved we could do this before we were ready.

I could do this. I had no choice but to do this.

Soft coos had me turning to my open balcony doors. I would have missed the snow-white owl with how easily he blended into the dark winter landscape, if not for his stark yellow eyes and the black envelope held between his grey beak. I tiptoed toward him, careful not to spook the wide-eyed messenger, but before I could get too close, the owl dropped the envelope and flew away.

I checked the sky before returning to my room to find the moon had already disappeared. If Motti was back home, I only had minutes to spare.

Did he know that I'd be the one to wake the world this morning with the sun? After how I'd left him last winter solstice, would he even care?

Hersorth's howl had me jolting forward with a gasp.

Suddenly, every fear I'd had of the wolves barreled past my bones, rattling my soul. My hands trembled, making me wonder if my earlier calm was just shock.

"Get it together," I muttered as I struggled to pull out the paper. Soathag would catch me in two seconds if I continued like this.

I scanned the note quickly with raised brows, knowing who it was from the first word.

Sunbeam,

Do you know I've watched you dance on your balcony morning and night since we were ten?

At first, it was another reason to hate you. It was as if you were tormenting me with how effortlessly everything came to you. You don't even realize you do it— stop the world as you dance. The clouds slow, the birds quiet, and time stills to watch you paint the sunrise and sunset.

But the older we grew, I realized you did it to calm your nerves while Edona left in the morning and returned in the evening. It helps to focus on something else when the fear threatens to drown you. Selfishly, watching you dance became as much of a helping habit for me as it has been for you.

I knew something was wrong when you

weren't on the balcony, preparing to dance.

No one gave me encouraging words when Father passed. In truth, because no one knew what to say or how to help. Even if there were words, I wouldn't have listened, knowing no matter what, my time had come.

They stopped checking on me a few weeks after transitioning, and I knew it was because of how well I held myself together. They'll do this to you, too, because you'll give no reason for concern, as you always try so hard to do. Instead, they'll whisper about how gracefully you took Edona's position, and they'll praise you loudly tonight at the celebration. And we'll smile and endure, for it's our job to comfort the world. To show them we will not falter and we will survive this tide of wolves.

These words may not hold merit now, but I hope they help when you tire of the chase.

Edona was one of the best sun goddesses in history. She was brave, cunning, and beautiful. But you will be the one they all remember. You are not the one who carries the sun each day but the sun itself. No tide can staunch your flame, for you are the light

when all others disappear. And you are the
most stubborn, presumptuous brat I have
ever met—this is why I know you'll make
Soathag regret you.

Everything will change now, and I
understand how terrifying the unknown seems.

I will never blame you for not feeling
how I feel, and I understand if you never
will. I only confess my love for you now so
I can be selfish one last time:

Push aside your fear. Survive long enough
to dance with me tonight.

Make it to tonight, Sunbeam, and I
swear the rest of the days will be survivable.

If they're not, I'll help you.

I may only be a moth, but I will follow
your blazing light each night with pride. I
will gladly orbit you from now until the end.

Just please survive.

For Edona. For Ilo. For me.

-M

I re-read Motti's letter while Mother's horses— my
horses—- led us out of the stables.

My hands no longer trembled when I folded the letter
and tucked it into my golden gown. My purpose was
inevitable. And I was beginning to accept that Motti and I

might be, too. I could not run from what I feared and loved. I no longer wanted to.

I LEANED AGAINST MY IRON CHARIOT, FOLLOWING Brenna's path as she lowered back into the mountains.

She had risen with fury, surprising Soathag with how fast she moved. It didn't take long for him to understand it was not Edona in the sky. I'm sure anyone else who paid attention to the chase had noticed something different about how the sun moved, too, and by tonight, everyone would know of Edona's quiet transition into Helan's realm.

I should have waited to meet Brenna down in the valley with everyone else, but I knew what coming back down for the first time was like. I had crumpled into a ball seconds after returning the moon to its resting place. I stayed there for hours, unable to move or breathe, while I let the mountains soak up my tears and grief. Tonight, if she needed me, I'd be here to hold her burdens, just as I vowed last winter and in my letter this morning.

Soathag was quick on her heels as her horses zigzagged through the clouds towards me. His howl shook the frosted rocks around me, causing my horses to shift with anticipation.

"The world's new little Sun Goddess races as she dances: Raw and unabashed."

Hálkon's voice had me straightening with a scowl.

He wore a suit, nearly identical to mine, in black velvet. His black hair was unkempt, blowing in two directions from the cold winter breeze. He studied me with cool calculation while tilting his head to look at my chariot.

My fists clenched at my sides. "You have some nerve to

be here."

Hálkon scoffed as he neared my chariot. "Why, because I'm not a god?"

"You know why," I snapped.

He reached out a finger to lazily touch the iron, and my horses again shuffled with nervous whinnies as if they, too, could feel the unwelcome tension he brought.

"What sort of gods are you anyway?" Hálkon huffed. "You only help to carry what creates balance in this world. Beyond that, you're nothing. Have you ever thought of that, Motti? What would you be like without your precious moon?"

I gritted my teeth. "What do you want?"

"Such a loaded question." He clucked his tongue against his teeth. "For a god, you act so mortal. Finding solace in friendships. Spilling your darkest secrets and desires to anyone willing to listen."

"We were friends, Hálkon. I trusted you."

I was twelve when I found him in these mountains. I had snuck out to explore and found him not far from here, playing by himself. We had written to each other ever since, helping one another, sharing jokes and stories, until he suddenly stopped.

It had taken everything in me not to kill him when he stood beside Brenna last winter solstice. He had been my friend, only to disappear and emerge with her in his arms.

I shook my head, desperate to understand. "You knew. You knew I've always loved her. Why the games? What did I ever do to you?"

Hálkon chuckled while joining me to lean on the chariot, but it rolled forward with the horses' skittish shuffles. I gave them a puzzling glance before checking for Brenna.

When I looked back at Hálkon, he studied me with hungry, glittering eyes. "The game is love, Motti. And you do not understand it. You wrote of love as if it was this all-consuming force of nature. But do you know it is far more dangerous to thirst for something always out of reach? To lust for what you cannot have, no matter how hard you try? That sort of longing brings an aching hunger. An insatiable, festering desire that can only be filled with your obsession." His lips curled into a malicious grin. "I grew tired of my hunger while you constantly whined for something within your grasp. Something you were too cowardly to take, so I did it instead. Brenna's love was so easy to chase." Hálkon clapped his hands together, making me flinch. "So easy to catch."

"But you didn't catch her, Hálkon."

He tilted his head and looked up. "That hardly matters now, little Moon God." My horses ran forward, eager to get away from him, already having figured out what I was desperately trying to comprehend. Without the chariot to lean on, we straightened to face one another as Hálkon continued, "To think, the two of you could have so easily had what my brother and I have always chased. If only she hadn't been so stubborn in her ways." Hálkon hummed, the sound rippling from his shoulders with graveled tones. "I think it's time we show her how it feels to lose the game."

Halkon's black suit was melting into a mass of shadows, covering him entirely. A familiar growl tore through the center of the sudden midnight cloud. I turned and ran to my chariot. I didn't need to witness my old friend's true form. The howl that haunted my family for centuries gave me confirmation as it crawled over me with cold, calculating revelation.

Before I could reach my panicked horses, Hersorth's

howl shook the ground beneath me. I tripped and rolled through the snow before sitting up to witness the wolf who killed my father. The wolf that had tricked me for years.

Hersorth leaned back on his haunches, his haunting golden eyes narrowing on me. He was half a field away, growing larger in black fur and shadow with every panicked breath I sucked in.

The night wolf's lips pulled into a sinister smile as he growled, "This ends now."

A sudden bright light flashed between us and I lifted my hand to shield my eyes as Brenna halted to a stop.

"You're right," Brenna panted. "It does."

Hersorth barked with irritation but wasted no time to race for her instead.

I stood, running forward with Brenna's name on my lips as she turned her horses to face Hersorth head-on.

She raced forward despite my rasping plea, Hersorth's maw opening wider and wider, focused on her and her horses.

Before Hersorth could touch her, Brenna swerved sharply to the left. Her chariot tipped on its side with the sudden jerk, causing her and the sun to roll out from the chariot's hold.

The sun barreled into Hersorth before he could correct his landing and the wolf yelped as it rolled with him. The night wolf clawed at the bright ball, desperate to escape as the fire licked its way up his paws and haunches. Struggling to get the ball of light off him, he let out a pained howl.

And another howl answered.

Just as Hersorth pushed the flames away from him, a flash of white barreled into his side. Soathag, who had been aiming for the sun, latched onto Hersorth with centuries of hunger in his bite.

I ran for Brenna and helped her stand as Hersorth and Soathag fought one another. We backed away, holding one another as the sound of gnashing teeth and crazed barks grew frenzied.

White and black fur blurred together, making it hard to see who was winning. Soathag and Hersorth howled in unison, and the ground around us shook from the pained harmony. A haunting crack sounded above from the shake, and I turned to see a sheet of snow sliding down the side of the mountain toward us.

Hersorth spoke of the need to fill his aching hunger, not realizing it would be his demise as Soathag fought him for the sun, thinking this shadowed wolf would steal his one true love. It seemed Hersorth, despite his tricks and years of scheming, lost to the game he thought he knew better than anyone.

We raced for our chariots as the dust settled around the wolves, both dead from their vicious attacks upon one another.

I memorized the wolves' figures in awe as Brenna and I climbed into the clouds side by side. Soathag and Hersorth held onto one another, claws in each other's fur in a bloody embrace. The sun lifted of its own accord, quick to follow our ascension as if to celebrate the downfall of what had threatened its existence for centuries.

A warm hand grasped mine as our horses slowed. Brenna was radiant, her golden hair and bronze skin glowing with the sun floating behind her. I studied every inch of her form, never wanting to forget the memory of the Sun Goddess who had ended Soathag and Hersorth's reign.

"Motti!" Brenna's voice matched the surprise on her face as she pointed to something behind me.

I turned to where she pointed to see the moon lifting from the other side of the mountain as snow slid down it, filling the canyon we had just been in. I spared one last glance to the wolves before the snow buried them.

Brenna's voice cracked as she spoke, "Without the wolves, the sun and moon no longer need us." A tear ran down her cheek. "I only wish our parents could see this."

Grabbing her chariot, I pulled mine to hers to be closer.

I wiped the tear from her cheek, too busy memorizing her beauty to find words.

Brenna's eyes glittered with emotion as she teased, "What does inevitability look like now, moth?"

"Infinite." The hold on my reins tightened as I looked up at the sky, brightly lit in saturated blues and purples from the sun and moon. "It looks infinite."

Brenna groaned. "Great. Infinite lifetimes of tiring over you."

"Here's to hoping, Sunbeam."

The Sun Goddess lifted her chin and laughed and gods, it was the most freeing sound I had ever heard. I had loved her laugh before, but the sound she had just made was triumphant in its call. I had never truly felt like a god until now, knowing that laugh was finally only for me. I mirrored her smile and began planning a thousand different ways to hear that joyous sound again.

Brenna urged her horses to race forward, and I gave a surprised chuckle before racing after her.

Like a moth chasing his flame, we danced through the sky with victorious cheers and taunts to one another, knowing there would never be another Sun and Moon God raised to fear the weight of the wolves.

HEART OF ICE SOUL OF FIRE

BY JADE CHURCH

Heart of Ice, Soul of Fire

My curiosity had gotten the better of me once again.

We had all heard the tales of the ice maiden, trapped in her castle by her own magic. Children's stories, a myth to explain our perpetual frosty climate, unchanged by the seasons. It was said that it was not always so, that the summers in Elondoria were long and hot and the autumns rich with colour.

It had been so long that nobody living could remember such a thing.

Ice and snow were in our blood, were more than just mere *weather*, they were a way of life. Still, even the most experienced of us could get caught out when it came to the late-year storms.

My horse had fled about three gales back, throwing me from its back in its panic as the white flakes grew heavier and the ice seemed to triple on the ground. Twice we'd slipped, and when the wind screamed louder in our ears, the mare'd had enough.

Elondoria had made living among the snow an art,

carving it and wielding it until it became something of use. Our bodies had slowly adjusted to the cold, our weapons changing to hunt for different game, and yet still I'd been foolish enough to ignore the warnings of the grey clouds and wandered out in search of rare prey that was only found this time of year—the arctic bear.

That bear would be my undoing, despite never having seen it.

What I needed was shelter, badly. My eyes were streaming from the cold and the water froze to my cheeks and lashes almost instantly as flurries of snow were sucked into my nose and melted in my mouth. I'd long lost feeling in my fingers and toes and, if not for the small kernel of magick I possessed, I would have been certain to have lost them from frostbite. As it was, the sputtering ember of fire in my blood was just enough to keep my blood moving, my heart pumping, but if I couldn't find somewhere to wait out this storm my magick would eventually fail.

Perhaps it would have been better to succumb to the storm.

I couldn't tell if it was due to the elements themselves, making me wander farther off the woodland trail than ever before, or if there was some kind of magick involved... But the fortress that loomed up ahead did not cast a shadow, instead blending into the snow as the frost on its walls glinted in the remaining sunlight. The gates did not squeak, swinging open with ease, and when I ran to the grand door on unsteady feet, my footprints barely disturbed the snow.

These were the details that I barely noticed, more concerned with getting inside before the storm could rage around me any harder, swallowing me whole. Perhaps I should have questioned my good fortune just a little more, hesitated at the threshold instead of diving in, but all I cared about was that my eyes were finally free of wind and ice.

With the door shoved closed behind me in an oddly muffled thump, the sounds of the tree branches clashing faded. The house was still, the air undisturbed, but the wood of the bannister around the sweeping staircase was dripping. The soft plunk of the droplets sent shivers down my spine and I remained in the doorway as I took in the dark room.

"Hello?" I called, my voice cracking and lips splitting, like I'd been moments away from joining the ice outside the house. "I'm sorry to intrude, only I was caught in a storm and yours is the first shelter I've found."

Nobody answered, no footsteps sounded, all remained quiet. I glanced to my left and saw a sitting room that looked long untouched. Was this place, this fortress, truly abandoned?

The floorboards beneath my feet felt springy as I made my way to the room, hoping it may have a grate for a fire so I could truly warm myself. Instead, I found a piano tucked into the corner on the far left, and what had once been plush armchairs curved around to face the instrument. No sign of a fireplace.

I backed out of the room, something about the way the chairs were positioned making me think of wraiths and specters.

Past and behind the stairs lay another doorway. This room was smaller than the first, with a large fireplace and ornate gilding placed front and center in the room. I hurried over and inspected the pile of wood inside a shiny golden bucket. It seemed dry enough, and I didn't have much other option, so I piled the wood into the grate and used the last dregs of my magick to get the fire burning.

Soon the cheery pops and crackles of the flames filled the room and I relaxed in a soft armchair with my feet propped up on a stool.

The storm had only just started to settle into the atmosphere when I'd found the house, so I had no way of knowing how long it would last. Sometimes the storms at this time of the year were fleeting, blowing in at full-force and wreaking havoc and destruction. Other times they could last days, and the cold chill that swept through the town was often more deadly than the high winds and shards of ice falling from the heavens.

Assuming I might have to hole up here for a few days, I knew I needed to check my surroundings and make sure there wasn't anything unwanted lurking within the shadows. Despite the emptiness of the house, it all seemed to be well-kept. The most obvious signs of disuse was the darkness, the musty smell of air gone stale, and the water that dripped from most places in the house, like it had been under ice for a century and was finally melting.

The stairs barely creaked when I made my way up them a few hours later, when my fingers and toes had pinked up and the trembling that had wracked my frame had eased. I wondered how long it would take for my sisters or my parents to notice I was missing? I'd told no one about this trip, knowing they'd try to dissuade me, but this would be my last chance to hunt and capture an arctic bear for this year, winning me the recognition of the entire town. Pride. Arrogance. I was starting to think they were not worthwhile causes to risk one's life.

The upstairs held many rooms, all immaculately presented as if for guests. Whoever had lived here must have had money beyond my imagination, given the richness of the fabrics and the purity of the crystal glasses by the beds. I could have my pick of sleeping chambers, and perhaps anything else in the house, I mused. I hadn't caught myself an arctic bear, but this place, lost to time as it seemed to be, could be almost as valuable.

I came to the final bedroom and was surprised to find my breath fogging the air. The shiny door handle was so cold it burned when I attempted to turn it and I stopped, hesitating. I could just pick one of the other rooms, I reasoned, I didn't need to check the inside of this one. Except, this was me and, as my mother had always told me, my curiosity had always been my downfall. I needed to know what was inside. It may even hold the key to the answers of what had befallen this place, why it had been hidden away amongst the snow, revealed only by the storm.

I reached into my back pocket and pulled on my thick glove before reaching again for the handle. There was a sharp crunching sound as I forcefully twisted it and pushed my shoulder against the door. It flew open and I stumbled inside, skidding slightly on the icy floor as I clung to the wood beneath my hands to right myself.

Slightly steadier, I dropped my hands and turned to survey the room before freezing in place. There was a woman here, probably no older than me. She stood in the center of the room, looking out at the world through the open curtains.

"I'm so sorry!" I swallowed hard and was ready to bolt, except something seemed strange. The woman didn't move. Not a hair drifted out of place, her shoulders still, and the frost on the floor spread out in a spiral from her form as if she exuded the cold. "Are you alright?"

I moved a little closer, taking care of my steps lest I lose my grip on the slippery surface again. I reached out a tentative hand, looking paler than usual in the cold white light of the storm outside, and gasped when it brushed the edge of the woman's shoulder.

Cold. Freezing. She was just like ice.

"Oh gods," I breathed, recoiling. *I should never have come here.* The thought was so loud in my mind it almost felt like it wasn't my own, and yet I found myself stepping closer and admiring the whorls in the ice that coated the woman's bare arms. Her skin was almost pearlescent, shimmering slightly when I tilted my head to better examine them. I lightly traced a finger over a perfectly imprinted snowflake on the back of her arm, the white sheen on her pale skin smudging and then instantly recovering. It was some kind of elemental magick, not unlike my own, but was this a curse? Or did the magick belong to this unknown woman? Frozen in time in her own home and overwhelmed by the clear power that maintained the ice encasing her?

I sighed, shaking my head as I pulled my hand back and away. It was more than pity surging inside me, it was anger too. Elondoria had learned a lot these past centuries, including how to properly wield magick safely... rather than persecuting those who showed any sign of it. From the style of this house, its riches untouched, I had to imagine that this woman, whoever she was, had not been so lucky as me to be born in a more progressive time. Even so, I'd struggled.

Angling my boots to keep my grip, I carefully stepped around the woman until I could see her face. She looked regal with her long nose and delicately pointed chin. I took an involuntary step closer, examining the strange blue-grey of her eyes barely visible beneath the snowflakes that swirled in them. My own eyes stung watching them move. Whatever this was... it was an active magick. If I stayed at the house, was I also at risk of becoming trapped in this state? Surely if that was the case I would have noticed adverse effects by now.

Her skin was bone white and tinged with blue around the edges, dark brows tipped with ice and serious mouth frowning slightly even in death.

I placed my hand to the skin of her chest, just below her throat. "I'm sorry," I murmured, my words filling the room in a way that felt stifling after such barrenness. "I'm sorry," I said again, barely above a whisper, and shuddered when my veins buzzed with a surge of power that raised the hairs on my skin.

My legs flew out from under me as I jumped backwards, the ice on the floor providing a slick surface that threatened to drag me down. I blew out a long breath before using the edge of the window sill to pull myself up and eye the frozen woman warily. She hadn't moved, the winter of her skin unchanged, but when I cautiously approached I shook my head in disbelief.

The delicate skin above the neckline of her formal dress fluttered ever so slightly, like my warmth, my magick, had jolted her heart into life. I pressed two fingers to the space that vibrated lightly and then dropped them just as fast. Her heart was beating. *Impossible.*

This woman who'd been abandoned in this house, locked inside her own body in an icy prison for years, was *alive.*

I SAT WITH HER. I COULDN'T GO BACK TO SITTING by the fire, in her house, knowing she was upstairs clinging to life and alone, as she must have been for some time now.

Whether she knew it or not, the frozen woman had saved my life. If I could return the favour somehow, then I was honour-bound to do so—but beyond duty or honour, I *wanted* to help her.

So I grabbed a blanket from one of the spare rooms, pulling it messily off of the bed and thinking that the disarray was good—it made the house feel more alive. Then I wrapped it around her shoulders and carefully lifted her. She weighed nothing, like she was more insubstantial than air, and it unnerved me. This magick had overtaken her to the point that she had almost faded out of existence, more ice than person. If not for the faint heartbeat in her chest, I would have thought this to be a hopeless endeavour.

I had settled back in front of the fire after positioning her in front of the other armchair, watching in fascination as the frost on her skin melted from the heat of the flames and immediately reformed. The thought occurred to me more than once that perhaps the myths were much more real than I'd imagined, than any of us had. Could this truly be the ice maiden of lore? Lost but not gone, trapped but not yet forgotten?

I peered into the flames, bracing my arms on my knees before pushing myself into a standing position and facing her. "Hello. Can you hear me?"

Nothing answered my words except the crackling of the fire and the sound of my own breathing. She didn't blink, or twitch, her stare blank and frosted.

"I don't know if you are cursed, or if this is a result of your own magick run wild, but if I can help you then I will." No change. I sighed, not really having expected anything else. So instead, I sat back down and began to tell her all of the things she had missed, the changes we'd made and the way Elondoria had progressed. I told her of my five sisters, Ansel, Leonie, Britta, Nimone, and Somer, and blinked into the distance for a moment when I realised that for all my rambling, I'd never given her my own name. "You must think me so rude," I mumbled before clearing my throat. "I hope that one day you will awake so I might learn your name in turn, but for now please call me Keir."

Movement in the corner of my eye had me stiffening, my hands instinctively clutching the arms of the chair as I whipped my head around and only knew my mouth had dropped open when the chill air tickled my tongue. The frozen woman, the ice maiden, was crying.

A long streak of water marred one perfect pale cheek, the ice hesitating to patch up the carved path, as if wavering, before the spirals of winter regained the upper hand and claimed the line of emotion.

"You can hear me," I said softly, wondering which part had made her cry. Or was she truly so bored of my storytelling that it had reduced her to tears? Exhaustion suddenly seemed to weigh down my body and I slumped in the chair, reaching blearily for the discarded blanket that I'd used to help carry the ice maiden down the stairs. "I promise, I'm going to help you."

The ice maiden didn't reply, but the flurries of snow in her eyes had melted and their smokey blue hue followed me into the comfort of my dreams.

TWO DAYS OF SNOW AND ICE, OF THE WIND howling and groaning as it tried to suck me out of the shelter I'd found and into its waiting, wrathful arms. The ice maiden's face and the tips of her fingers had entirely thawed the more I spoke to her of life in the town. Yet, still she herself still did not speak. And the longer I waited, the more impatient I grew, yearning to see what her lips may look like parted with breath, exhaling through a kiss, their full and curved glory tilted in a laugh.

Truthfully, I was enchanted. Not magickally, but rather in the ways of beauty and the heart. I wasn't sure I would have noticed if it had been five days that had passed us in the storm, but I couldn't—wouldn't—leave her even if I could. What if I left and then couldn't find my way back? What if, in my absence, she began to fully freeze over, her heart beat dropping, the mystery of her voice forever unknown?

The tilt of her dark brows convinced me that she was intelligent, their crooked angle a challenge, while the set of her shoulders radiated confidence. The hollow beneath her jaw spoke to me, telling me a thousand stories of determination, courage... love. My heart beat in time with the fragile tremble of her chest, like our very fates were intertwined. Had the storm led me to her on purpose? Was I meant to be here to help free her? For fate to intervene... Well, she had to be very special, indeed.

I'd ransacked the cellar and dug through the cupboards in the kitchen and pantry and had been relieved to find both wine, bread, cheese, and some kind of cured meat. Normally I wouldn't have touched it, assuming it to be stale or mouldy after so long hidden away, but if what I suspected was true, the perishables were likely just as fresh now as the day they'd been purchased.

Aside from being slightly damp from defrosting, the food had been fine. This only reaffirmed my theory that it was not only the maiden who'd been frozen, but the entire house itself. I posited my theory to her later in the evening on my third day in the house but saw no response. That was okay, I reasoned, she was still alive. There was still time.

I kept one eye on her pulse as I drank the fine wine straight from the bottle and continued where I'd left off earlier that day—the first time my magick had presented itself and the lessons I'd had to take afterwards to ensure my flames remained under my control.

"It must have been hard for you, not knowing what we now know, to live in the fear that you might hurt someone you love. Is that why you're the only one here? Where are your family? Your loved ones? Did they leave you here alone?" The bottle sloshed forcefully as I thudded it down onto the floor at my feet. "That's not your fault. They should have helped you, not abandoned you. But it's okay. I'm here, I can teach you control. And look—" I held out my palm in front of her, conjuring a flame big enough to light the wick of a candle. "—Our powers are two sides of the same coin. Fire and ice. If you'd just wake up, I'd be honoured to be your balance until you can stand on your own."

The flame in my palm winked out and I sat back down, exhaustion weighing my bones as I let the silence consume me. After a few moments of wallowing, I walked to the back of the room and drew back the deep burgundy curtain.

Outside, the world had vanished beneath a vast blur of white and grey. This close to the window, I could feel the wind rattling the panes and see fresh flurries swirled in perfect patterns blasting past. The storm was far from being over.

Drip. Drip. Drip.

I turned and watched the water descend from her

fingertips, running down the backs of her arms as the skin of her arms showed clearly.

My feet carried me towards her before I registered making the decision. Tentative fingers curled around chilled palms and a shudder wracked through me. This was *her* power. She had to be the one to relinquish it, else she may retaliate instinctively and the progress we'd made would be lost. Blasting her with my flames would prove to do more harm than good.

I squeezed her fingers with my own and waited to see if I could feel any kind of response from her, disappointed when none came.

"I believe in you," I murmured into her ear, hoping the warmth of my breath might trigger something inside of her. "I'll wait as long as it takes. You've waited long enough. Whatever penance it is you think you are serving, let it now end. Come and see how Elondoria thrives. The snow, the ice, we are its masters and so, too, are you."

I settled back into my armchair by the fire and didn't say another word, just sipped my wine in silence and let her think over what I'd said. I couldn't help her if she didn't want to help herself.

I awoke in the armchair when a *THUMP* rang out. It had been quiet for so long, the small sound might as well have been a roll of thunder and I instinctively leapt up and out of the chair only to falter.

"You-You're awake." My voice was croaky and I swallowed twice as my shock turned into relief. "*You're awake.*"

The sound had been the maiden's knees hitting the

ground, the last of her ice having dissolved into a puddle around her feet. The muscles in her arms shook, unable to bear her weight as she attempted to stand.

"Here," I said quietly and then stumbled forward to lift her into the chair I'd just vacated.

"No!" Her voice was hoarse and higher than I'd imagined it would be. "Don't touch me. Get back!"

I immediately let go and she toppled into the armchair with force, sending it rocking backwards until she tumbled out of the seat, peering at me from around the edges like I could spring at her at any minute. I held up my hands placatingly and then sat down, straight into the puddle of icy water she'd left behind. Wincing, I shuffled over on the floor and clearly looked pathetic enough that the maiden decided I wasn't truly a threat.

"I'm not going to hurt you."

Her eyes widened and a laugh tore its way free from her throat. "Hurt... *me?*" I frowned when she continued to laugh before the rough sound cut off. "Do you know who I am? What you've done in waking me?"

I stood up and brushed down my trousers for errant dust. "I didn't wake you."

"You lit the spark," she hissed and I raised an eyebrow.

"You fueled the flame," I countered. "As for who you are, I've been dying to know."

Her grey-blue eyes flashed at me from across the room and ice spread out from beneath her fingertips on the floor. Her face blanched as she glanced down and caught sight of it, pulling her hands away abruptly.

"Your name," I reminded her, and she pulled her eyes away from the evidence of her lapse in control to stare at me. "Breathe," I commanded. "What is your name?"

The breath she loosed rattled but her jaw was tight,

resolute, when she replied. "I am Princess Nixias of Elondoria, first in line to the throne, bearer of frost and ice."

I inclined my head. "Pleased to meet you."

Her lip twitched and I wanted to grin at the sight of the glimpse of emotion. "And you are?"

"Don't pretend you don't remember my name," I taunted and colour flushed high on her cheekbones.

"Keir," she whispered and I smiled. "You have condemned my people to death in waking me."

"How so?"

"My magick… it is deadly. A curse."

I reached deep within me and let my own magick unfurl, rising from my skin in a wave of tightly controlled flame, and her mouth dropped open. I let the flame dissipate and she shook her head in disbelief, her white hair drifting in the wave of heat my flames had created in the room.

"How?" she said, voice choked and I moved to her, righting the armchair and offering her a hand up that she hesitantly accepted.

"Time. Practice."

She shook her head again, but I didn't think it was in denial—more like shock.

"Elondoria has changed much since you've been gone, Princess."

"Nix," she murmured and I bit my lip on a smile.

"Nix."

"And what of the throne? M-My descendants?"

I shrugged as I stoked the fire in the grate and then reached for the wine I'd left unfinished before I'd fallen asleep. "It's been unclaimed for as long as I've known. Where are your family? What happened to you?"

I handed her the bottle and she looked at it for a second before drinking straight from it. "I lost control," she said simply and my heart hurt for her. It didn't have to be this way. Magick was a gift, not a curse, if her family—her *kingdom*—had just helped her, all of this could have been avoided. "Did you mean what you said to me? About being my balance?"

My pulse leapt. I knew she'd heard me. "Yes."

"Will you show me?"

"I'll show you the world," I whispered before drinking deeply from the bottle she passed back to me. "And I'll protect both you from it and it from you."

Nix nodded, her eyes on the fireplace but her mind clearly elsewhere. "But maybe we should stay here a while longer, if you don't mind another meal of cheese and bread."

I snorted. "As you please, Your Majesty."

Her lips moved, forming the title as if only just realising she was a princess no longer. "Tomorrow, then."

"Tomorrow."

WE
WARM
THE
STARS

BY JENNA WEATHERWAX

WE WARM THE STARS

THE FISHMONGER'S DAUGHTER LOOKED UP AT THE winter sky, watching the stars above. The sky seemed deeper than normal.

Her back against the thick layer of still-falling snow, she stared up and up for hours on end. The stars glinted above, their shapes familiar to her. Colors blended together at the seams, too, beautiful blues and greens blurring in waves as true winter approached. Warm as she was in her thick wool coats and fur mittens and seal hide boots, her skin burned with the freezing air wherever she was exposed to it.

The stars, she noted distantly to herself, having to concentrate to hear her thoughts over the shrieking wails of her mother from inside the house, *must be cold, too.* They had no fur or hide to curl up into, and the earth, she imagined, must look so cold, covered in the swirling white blizzard.

Her father had told her the stories of the stars, when she was young. The creatures that lived in the night sky, their tragic and hopeful origins, their ascension and fame. She could follow the lines of their shapes easily now, and knew their names. The Hunter, the Ram, the Harp, the Dragon and, her favorite, now brighter than any others, the Great Bear. It was easy to find her, eyes drawn to the simple outline in both winter and summer.

"Are you, too, cold?" the fishmonger's daughter asked the stars, eyes on the bear. "Are you, too, lonely?"

Snowflakes fell around her, the softest of sounds as they landed. The stars sparkled above her and the fishmonger's daughter caught her breath and, as the world seemed deeper and wider, as the winter made silent the earth, she strained her ears to listen for a response. For a small moment, the stars hesitated, as if opening their mouths to answer, when another piercing screech cracked across the serene space, like ice on a frozen lake.

"Girl!" Her grandfather's voice snapped out, following the violent sound of the door thrown open. "Inside, now! Your mother needs you."

The fishmonger's daughter spared a final glance at the stars.

To them, she murmured, "I'm sorry. I must go. Stay warm."

The stars twinkled their answer, but it was lost to the falling snow.

THE GROUND WAS TOO FROZEN FOR A REAL funeral. Instead, they lit a pyre with the last of their firewood.

Her grandfather did not shed a tear. He had never liked her father, thinking the fishmonger nothing more than a poor man with only his trade to keep their family afloat.

And now there was nothing, nothing but smugness as the old man was proven right.

Her mother did not stop crying, not as her father's body burned and not after. Awful sounds, round with grief, filled their home. The sobs bounced between bending, splitting beams and cold, rotting floorboards. The only sturdy structure, her new sister's crib, rocked with matching cries, the babe scared and cold without her mother's touch.

There were some rations to get them through the winter with her father's fishing. But not many. Not for four mouths to feed. The hearth stayed lit, but only enough to keep the coals alive. It would not last for long.

"What will we do?" wailed her mother, again and again. The fishmonger's daughter rocked her sister in her arms, attempting to soothe her empty stomach and freezing fingers. She could hear the winter wolves howling, circling their home and waiting, waiting. She kissed the little fingers, humming a song easily lost to her mother's question, asked again and again, "What will we do?"

"Did I not tell you?" Her grandfather yelled in response, two pints of ale filling his stomach and his mind. "A poor man loves well while alive, but leaves behind only graves—"

The fishmonger's daughter flinched at the words, but said nothing. She hummed, swaying. Her sister's cheeks were red, but her fingers were the color of the lilacs in the south in the summer, almost bruised with the cold.

Her mother cried out, "What will we do?"

Her grandfather snorted derisively, spilling the vile liquid over his chest. "And what a fool! Even I could've told you the ice would crack—"

She hummed louder. Her sister wailed, wiggling against her thin blanket.

Her mother pleaded, "What will we do?"

Then, her grandfather was yelling. "And now! Now, we'll freeze to death because you picked a foolish man to marry!" He threw down his cup, and it shattered on the floor. "Now we will die! What did I tell you?"

Her mother's only answer remained the same, voice echoing around them, "*What will we do?*"

As if in answer, there was a knock on the door.

Her mother's cries stopped. Her grandfather's bitter words halted. Even the babe's wails quieted for a moment. The fishmonger's daughter frowned, staring at the simple plank of wood on their door.

Their home was no more than a fishing shack, just on the edge of a lake and miles from the closest village. The snow came in wild flurries, now, and no man wishing to live would dare make the long trek to their creaking and trembling home.

Her grandfather pushed himself to his feet, staggering to the door. He wrenched it open, the wood slamming against the walls. He was a large man, his shoulders entirely blocking the howling wind, bitting air, and the view of their visitor.

"Who are you?" her grandfather barked out.

The fishmonger's daughter did not expect the sound of a woman's voice, cool and soft as the falling snow. "May I come in?" The pretty voice asked. A pause. "I am quite cold."

"We have no food," her grandfather snapped. "Not for us, let alone guests—"

"Let her in," the fishmonger's daughter interrupted, speaking for the first time since she'd spoken to the stars.

Her mother's head snapped toward her, surprise on her face, and so did her grandfather's. She cleared her throat, shifting the babe in her arms, and repeated herself. "Let her in. It's cold out there."

Before her grandfather could respond, a pale hand pushed him aside. The first thing the fishmonger's daughter saw was white. A cloud of it spread out behind the guest,as if she was carrying the winter on her shoulders.

It was only when the woman stepped in front of her grandfather did she see the head of the cloak, the dark eyes of an icebear staring at her from atop the woman's head, a row of pure white teeth hanging down to her brows.

Gray eyes met hers, and she opened her mouth to greet their guest, when her grandfather spoke again.

"Who are you?" the old man demanded.

The woman did not move her gaze from the fishmonger's daughter, speaking slowly and softly enough that the fishmonger's daughter leaned forward to hear her words. She was a beautiful woman, upon closer inspection. Long, dark hair hung in thick braids down to her soft waist, interspersed with silver strands that caught the candlelight. Her face was soft, the gentle curves of a childhood sledding hill and the rosiness of a spring bud.

"I come with an offer," the woman said to her instead of answering him.

The fishmonger's daughter frowned. "An offer?"

"Tell me," she murmured, a pale ghost of a smile on her face. She took a step closer and the fishmonger's daughter had to look up and up. She was tall, broader than the entire home, it felt like. And, despite her next words, she radiated warmth from beneath her thick cloak. "Do you know the tradition of the Ice Wife?"

She blinked. She did not. But, from the outraged sound her grandfather made, he seemed to recall it.

"You cannot take the fishmonger's daughter." His voice was an order, his fist slamming against the table. Her mother began to sob again. So did the baby.

The woman ignored him, waiting for a response from her.

She shook her head. "I do not."

The woman nodded. "It is an old tradition. In exchange for protection," her icy eyes flickered to the house, to her mother, to the babe in her arms. "A woman warms a bed for the winter." Another small smile. "It is cold, after all."

"Protection?" the fishmonger's daughter asked, frowning in her confusion.

"A warm place to stay," the woman clarified, eyes flickering to the shaking home with a soft frown, then to the empty shelves, and the pathetic fire. "Food for the long months. Wood for your stove and your hearth." Her eyes returned to brown ones, a dancing humor in them, now. "Protection from wolves and bears."

"It sounds like a dream."

The woman laughed, then, the sound like dripping icicles. "It does."

Her grandfather huffed, pounding his fist again. "You cannot take—"

"I take nothing," the woman finally addressed him, her voice whistling through their home sharply. She bared her teeth and, just for a moment, it looked like the bear of her cloak did, too. "That doesn't care to be taken."

The words brought an unexpected warmth to her face. She must've made some sort of noise, because the woman turned back to her. Quieter, she explained, "It is not an order, sweet fishmonger's daughter. It is an offer. My bed, your family's protection."

"Just for the winter?" she asked, blinking up at her.

The woman nodded, resolute. "Just for the winter." The woman reached out, then, and tucked a mousy brown curl behind her ear. "This is my offer. Do you need time to consider?"

She hesitated, eyes going to the squalling babe for just a moment. She gave the child back to her mother.

"No," she answered the woman. "I accept."

The woman's smile was wide and white and sharp. "I am pleased." She looked away, then, at the house, at her family, and nodded as if deep in thought. "Tonight, pack whatever you wish to bring. I will return tomorrow night."

She nodded, swallowing. "Do I–should I–prepare anything? To bring?"

The woman's face softened, taking the fishmonger's daughter's hand in her own. She brought it to her lips, brushing a dry kiss across her knuckles. She shivered with it, eyes level now as the woman leaned down. Her breath caught in her lungs, cheeks swirling with heat.

"Prepare nothing," the woman responded, careful with her words. "Only yourself."

"Tomorrow?" she asked as her hand was lowered.

The woman nodded, moving past her grandfather, moving past their door.

Her words were a promise. "Tomorrow. Sleep well, sweet fishmonger's daughter."

She slept well. Her mother exhausted herself with her tears and her grandfather passed out on his chair at the table, so the house was quiet but for the creaking of the wood and howling of the wind. She dreamt, that night, for the first time in a long while. She dreamt of blinking stars and bears running across the horizon and the crunch of fresh snow between her tongue and palate, tasting somehow of honey.

Sleep was sweet, but she woke up to her mother's screaming. Drowsily, she wiped the sands of sleep from her eyes, question on her lips, but, when her vision cleared, she, too, gasped loud enough to wake the sleeping.

Their home was transformed. No longer creaking or shaking or trembling in the wind, the thin wood had been replaced with thick, sturdy logs. The beams across the ceiling now displayed intricate carvings of the same stories her father had recited, the creation of the stars. Fire, burning yellow with fragrant smoke, lit the room in the morning light, illuminating the quartz in the river stones that now lined the walls. The windows filled the rest of the space, heavy velvet curtains tied around them to keep the warmth in and the chill out.

Their small kitchen, last night no more than a couple of empty shelves and her grandmother's pots and pans, was now bathed in the sun from a skylight. It caught the shiny skin of fresh produce and meats, as well as dried food, too. Flour and yeast, sugar and salt, and even sweet confections lined the shelves.

The only thing unchanged was the baby's crib. Only, the bedding that lined it was soft cotton and knitted toys, and the baby's laughter filled the space more fully than the smells of spices or the light of the sun or the sounds of her mother's screaming.

She was on her feet before she could think twice, but she stopped to see that the torn rags she'd fallen to sleep in was now a thick, flannel nightdress. Even her toes, which poked out of holey socks the night before, stayed warm in wool stockings.

The fishmonger's daughter cried, then, unsure how to understand this miracle. She spent the morning in tears, the afternoon sampling every sweet treat with her mother, the evening tracing the patterns of the mantel place and listening to her mother's happy cries and her grandfather's snores after drinking the sweet wines. Dinner was more elaborate than anything she'd ever had, bursting with flavor across her tongue.

"Thank you," her mother said, embracing her for the first time in a long time. She held her back, nodding into her mother's bosom, just as she had needed since her father died. Her mother continued, "I do not care if she is a witch or a monster, you have saved us. Thank you."

The thought was not one that occurred to her, yet, but, now spoken, her joy morphed into trepidation and, then, as the sun sank into its own golden light, fear. Night was here, now, and the stars flickered above them, watching and waiting.

She knew of witches, of course, and their tricks. Her father's stories mentioned them, too. Bread crumbs and boiling pots for fat children and cackling laughter, they fed off the stories of the hungry and scared and—

There was a knock on the door.

She took a step, hand on the doorknob, and paused. The woman had kept her promise, and now it was time for her to keep her own. But what waited for her, outside her home? A season alone with a stranger, at the very least. How would she spend her days? As a servant? As a prisoner?

Her cheeks bloomed pink, as she remembered the brush

of lips on her knuckles. As a lover, perhaps? She was unmarried, but she was not entirely uneducated. She knew what a pretty fishmonger's daughter might be asked to do, as she warmed a man's bed. But what of a woman?

Another knock, softer. She opened the door.

The woman smiled down at her. "Good evening. Are you ready to go?"

She opened her mouth to respond, but, before she could, her mother was throwing herself to her knees, sobbing out her thanks to the woman. The woman frowned, carefully stepping out of her reach with an expression of total neutrality.

"Stand," the woman told her, shaking her head with a grimace. "Save your gratitude for your daughter."

Her mother's tears stopped, confusion halting the flood. "What do you mean?"

The woman scoffed and did not answer, instead stepping around the supplicating mother and reached for the daughter's hand. "Tell me," the woman said again, that same imploring tone to the words as she nodded to their now grand household. "Does this satisfy my side of the offer?"

The fishmonger's daughter nodded, disbelieving still. "It does."

The woman smiled, stepping closer. "Are you ready to go, then?"

She hesitated, but only for a moment. This was her home and this was her family, but her father had raised her to be a just girl. A sale was a sale, a deal was a deal, even if she was the thing being dealt. Besides, she thought, listening to the baby coo instead of cry, they would be safe and warm, fed and happy in their new home. The fishmonger's daughter collected her small knapsack, filled only with the few, threadbare dresses she'd inherited, and looked to her family.

"May I say goodbye?"

The woman's eyes went soft. "Of course."

The fishmonger's daughter approached her sister first. Stepping up to the crib, she gently touched the tawny tuft of hair on her head. The babe gurgled a farwell and the fishmonger's daughter leaned over to press a kiss to her forehead. She spoke no words, but her heart ached with missing her already. How grown she would be, when the fishmonger's daughter returned.

To her mother, she tried to give her a brave smile. Her mother began to weep, the vitality of the sound renewed, as soon as she opened her mouth, but she patted her mother's head, and spoke, "Shh, it'll be okay. I'll be back soon, mother. Take care of the babe and I will see you in the spring." Just as she had done with the babe, she pressed a kiss to her forehead.

Her grandfather received no parting words.

She turned back to the woman and offered her hand. "Now I am ready."

The woman led her through the door, opening it for her. A blizzard waited for them outside, eager to embrace them with sharp winds and icy downpour. The fishmonger's daughter shivered with it, but even her trembling stopped when her eyes caught the sight before her.

Mahogany shone in the moonlight, the curves of the hand-carved sled stark against the white of the snow. Two lanterns illuminated its body, warm light pouring across the winter night. In front of the sled, two all-white elk huffed and stomped their heavy hooves into the powdery snow, waiting for their orders. Larger than any animals she'd ever seen, the fishmonger's daughter paused, afraid.

The woman saw her nerves and hummed. "Come."

Gently, the woman placed both their hands on the strong neck of the elk, and, even through the warmth of her mittens, the fishmonger's daughter could feel the softness of the elk's fur. The woman's voice was slow and soft, "They are good animals, you need not fear them. They are here to help us on our journey."

She could not help but be warmed by the words and, truly, there was peacefulness in the animals' eyes. The woman watched closely as she moved her hands over the fur, smiling when the fishmonger's daughter took a step closer and, quietly, she spoke to the animals.

"You are beautiful," she told the creatures. "And your fur is soft and thick. But, tell me, are you warm enough?"

The closest elk stomped its foot, snorting a hot breath into the night air. The fishmonger's daughter laughed, amused by its response, but, when she looked up to the woman, those colorless eyes met her own with a strange emotion swirling.

"Why do you ask?" the woman wondered, nodding to the elk. "They are creatures of the cold, after all. They were made for the winter. They were born in a blizzard. Why do you ask if they are warm?" Though the words were not meant to be an accusation, there was something stiff about them, almost too formal.

She blinked up at the woman. "Oh. I do not know. It just seems, to me, that someone ought to ask."

The expression, still a mystery to her, deepened. "Why? Why do you care if they are cold?"

She hummed her consideration. "The winter is hard. It is easier when someone cares." Her voice took on its own strange tone, a weariness creeping as her eyes fell from the woman's, reaching out to the great, white space surrounding her home. "And I suppose I am used to caring for everyone, anyway."

"And who cares for you?" the woman murmured, reaching out to touch one apple-blossom cheek.

Her head lifted and the blush deepened. Words dried on her tongue. "Well," she said after a long moment. "I take care of myself."

The woman was as silent as the snow falling, then she nodded and patted the closest elk on its back. "Come," she told her, stepping around her to reach the sled. Offering her hand, she said, "The journey is long and we must arrive by dawn."

She took her hand and the woman lifted her easily into the sleigh. Dense blankets of wool covered the seats, but, as the woman slid into the seat next to her, she pulled another blanket from the back of the sleigh, tucking it around her, tight and warm. Her lap, her legs, even around her feet, another blanket was wrapped tightly around her.

At her questioning look, the woman said, "It is cold and the wind will be sharp." And, then, the woman moved closer until their shoulders brushed and her breath caught in her lungs. Lifting her arm, the woman draped the icebear cloak over her shoulders, her strong arm pulling her closer so that the dense hide enveloped her in the bubble of warmth.

They were close enough that the clouds of their breathing merged, surrounding them.

"Tell me," the woman said, then, voice so gentle as they pressed together. "Are you warm enough?"

Warmth bloomed inside of her, nothing to do with the

temperature. It came out as a whisper, her answer. "I am very warm."

The woman smiled, then, and it was a blinding thing. Sun reflecting off the untouched banks.

"Very good," the woman responded, the black eyes of the bear glittering. She took the reins, gathering the attention of the elk, and nodded to the cloak around their shoulders. "If your eyes grow weary from the wind, duck down. If you grow tired, sleep. Once the animals begin their journey home," she paused, words deliberate. "It is difficult to slow them."

She nodded. She did not want to miss a moment of this journey, curious and awed by the night so far. Where would the woman take her? How long would they travel? How could she sleep through any of it? But, as she pulled the reins and the animals pulled them across the smooth snow, she was lulled by the swift and rhythmic music of their hooves against the ground, by the easy movement of the sleigh, by the warmth of the woman next to her.

Her eyes grew heavy as the air grew thinner. Before long, she was seeing the world through her own fluttering eyelashes, glimpses of the dark space around them, lit only by moonlight and dancing constellations. Snow crunched below the sleigh, a lullaby of a winter journey, and, though the fishmonger's daughter tried her best to stay awake, she found herself drifting asleep with her head on the woman's shoulder.

Vivid dreams danced in her mind as she slumbered. She imagined strange, new places, far beyond the reaches of the little fishing village, far beyond its ever-shrinking population and ever-growing sense of dread as the winters became colder and sharper every year. She imagined fantastical palaces of gemstone and precious metals, lawns of silk and soft cotton, horizons filled with light prisms of all undiscovered shades, and creatures of miraculous and nightmarish origins, stomping and crawling and flying over their crystal castles and amazing meadows.

Images swirled in her head of all these unbelievable worlds, their edges blurring as if they were sledding by them. She could scarcely comprehend one before the next was lost in their distance. The creatures all paused to watch her, in return, and their sharp eyes reflected her own amazement. Perhaps it was the magic of her new home or her fitful sleep or the terror of the unknown, but she seemed to sleep for nights upon nights, until the lullaby came to its end outside of her slumber.

She was woken up by a soft touch to her cheek and the woman's voice.

"Wake now, sweet girl. We have arrived." The words floated around her and it took her sleep-addled brain a moment to truly hear them and even longer to understand them. Once she did, she gasped awake, blinking away the sands of sleep to see the woman's pale face break into a smile as she began to unwrap the fishmonger's daughter from her layers of warmth. "Let me."

The fishmonger's daughter nodded, arms still securely held beneath the fabric. It gave her a moment to take in her new home for the winter, as the woman carefully exposed her body to the whipping winds. She gasped again as her eyes caught sight of the woman's home.

Just like the ones in her dreams, the palace seemed carved from crystal, the cloudy opalescence catching the first fires of the newborn sunrise in all its exact carved design. The windows and doors, especially, caught the golden warmth of the encroaching dawn, and, as she stared, it looked as if the interior of the palace held the sun itself.

The woman finished, releasing the fishmonger's daughter of her cotton holdings, and easily jumped out of the sled. Her boots did not sink an inch into the snow. No, it was as if she floated above the powder and glided over it. She held out a hand, the white fur of her magnificent cloak swaying in the breeze. All around them, drifts of swirling snow rolled through the endless fields.

"Come," the woman said again, a careful command. She took her hand, let her lift her easily out of the sleigh. The elk stomped, eager to find their own homes and the woman continued, "The dawn arrives soon. We should be inside, when it does."

Something was buried in the words, not quite fear, but certainly something urgent. She, seeing the incredible magic of her home's transformation and the palace before, was not eager to see what could inspire such a tone from the tall woman. She nodded, grabbing her only satchel, and let herself be guided through the impressive gates and the wide double doors.

The wind cracked around them, so strong that she thought, if she were to let go of the hand in hers, it would sweep her away. She shivered, the freezing sting of the air against her exposed face painful without the protection of the cloak and the layers of fabric. The woman frowned at her, pulling her along quicker.

As they both stepped out of the way, the elk kicked up a blizzard of their own, snorting and trotting as they pulled the sleigh around the house. The fishmonger's daughter attempted to watch them go but, between blinks, they disappeared into the clouds of their own making.

"Welcome," the woman said warmly as she pushed the doors open, "to my home."

The inside of the palace burned brilliantly and beautiful

warmth spilled across her face, kissing her like a long-lost lover. Despite the colorless chill of the season, the spirits of summer and spring danced across the crystalline floors of the palace. Her head spun as she looked from one amazement to another.

Fragrant flowers of unimaginable shades and shapes decorated the space, and candlelight poured from the transparent sconces on the walls, and sweet music filled the halls. Lush rugs of animal furs lined the walkways and tapestries with carefully embroidered stories colored the walls.

"And now," the woman added softly, closing the door behind them. "It is your home, too."

"It is beautiful," she confessed, eyes wide as she took it all in.

"Thank you," the woman answered, offering her arm She took it and was led through the glass halls. "Come. My servants will show you around tomorrow. For now," she continued as they came upon an impressive door and, inside, a grand bedroom waited for them. A tall bed with a hundred soft blankets and a mountain of goose-down pillows and silk sheets, all illuminated by the soft burning of the crackling fire. More tapestries covered the clear brick, depicting familiar stories of the constellations and trapping the delicious warmth in the walls. "We shall sleep."

She could only nod her agreement, pulled into the room. Rainbows danced in the walls and, despite the magic she had seen, or maybe because of it, suddenly, the fear from the night before returned. She was here, so far from her home and her family, with only her meager possessions, and the bed was big and loomed above her, surrounded by soft, white curtains, and she knew she would live there for this winter. But she didn't know what was expected of her.

"Tomorrow, I will show you how to start the fire," the woman told her, nodding to the hearth. "So you may stoke the flames this winter. But, for tonight, I have laid out your bedclothes." And she had. A pile of fabric waited for her on the foot of the bed, soft and thick and, as she held up the nightdress, she noticed it was just her size, as if made for her. "Dress and we shall sleep."

The woman sighed, then, rolling her shoulders for a moment before she divested herself of her fur-lined boots first, and then the thick outer pants, and the darkly dyed wool of her sweater. She left herself in only the thin material of her underclothes, the width of her shoulders and strength in her form undeniable, now, just as the curves of her chest and the breadth of her hips. A sliver of pale skin flashed as the woman stretched. The fishmonger's daughter gasped, turning away from the sight as the woman crouched to stir the fire.

Her fingers clutched the fabric of the nightgown tightly. She wanted to put it on, wanted out of her cold clothes and heavy coat, but the thought of stripping in front of the woman made her cheeks bloom. She hesitated, unable to ask but unable to obey. The woman noticed her pause, frowning at her.

"The washroom is through the doors," she told her simply. "Should you require privacy."

Swallowing heavily, she fled the room, closing the door behind her the moment she entered the washroom. The air was thick with steam, the humid air swirling around her, but she could still make out the intricately carved ivory and porcelain fixtures, the clawfoot bath and the wide sink and the flawless mirror.

Her reflection stared back at her as she removed her outer clothes and then the softer material against her skin.

There was no soft fat on her body to keep anyone warm, she thought as she stared at herself in the mirror for long moments. No, her lips were a touch lavender, and her hair was limp and her skin bruised around her eyes. Grief had exhausted her and, now, she was cold and alone and the fear of the unknown began to pound against her temples. Why was she here? What good could she do? How could she keep anyone warm, when she was made of only bones and grief?

A knock on the door. The fishmonger's daughter startled, nearly dropping the fine-woven fabric in her hands.

The woman's voice was soft. "Are you alright?"

Pulling the shift on swiftly and not sparing herself another glance, she answered the question by opening the door. The woman blinked down at her, surprised by the action, and her face transformed into a smile as she saw her in the gown.

"Do you like it?" the woman asked, curious.

She considered the question. It was beautiful, of course, the wool dyed a splendid saffron yellow. The fabric swam over her arms, breasts and hips like salt water, flowing down her thighs and down her legs. It was rich to the touch, soothing against her winter-rough skin, even as it protected against the cold air.

"Yes," she answered after a moment. "I love it. Thank you."

The woman's smile softened and, reaching out slowly, she brushed her thumb against her cheek.

"You are very welcome," she returned. Steam met the cold air of the bedroom and the tension was just as thick between them. The touch lingered and she opened her mouth to say something, to ask how the night would go, what the woman would want of her, but the woman's hand dropped before she could.

"Come," the woman said again, stepping back to allow her back in the room. "I am tired. Let us sleep."

The fishmonger's daughter followed, pausing only once she approached the bed. It was tall, lifted from the cold ground, and the coverings were loose and slippery. The woman noticed her struggle and, as she had all night, offered her a hand to guide her onto the bed. The sheets were cool, as she sank into the bedding. The woman followed after her, her height allowing her to easily slip between the sheets. Maybe it was the cloak, which still billowed around her shoulders, but she did not shiver.

"Lift," the woman said. She pulled the corner of the topmost blanket down and down until the fishmonger's daughter could slide under it. Their legs brushed, despite the size of the mattress, and the fishmonger's daughter's skin burned when they touched. She shivered again at the reminder of warmth, and she realized how cold she was. Perhaps grief was not the only reason her lips looked so blue and her skin pricked into goose pimples. It was winter, after all, and she was always cold.

The woman's face grew concerned, eyes raking over her body.

"Here," the woman said after a moment. "Come closer."

The fishmonger's daughter froze. Was this it, then? Would her duties as the woman's Ice Wife be fulfilled?

But the woman did not demand her body. She did not lift the blanket, but, just as she had in the sleigh, she opened her icebear cloak, ushering the fishmonger's daughter into the cloud of warmth around her body. Her teeth chattered and, despite how much she wanted it, she hesitated. The woman made a considering noise, but waited for her, keeping the cloak open. The fire crackled and she shivered one more time before diving into the promise of warmth in the woman's arms.

The icebear fur scratched against her skin, but the woman's body was a soft place to land. A strong arm curled around her, pulling her close, pulling their bodies together with her back to the woman's front, and the cloak draped over them both. She fit well here. Her head rested in the hollow of the woman's elbow. Only then did the woman pull the rest of the blankets over them both.

A swift gust of icy wind blew throughout the room and the candles only flickered once before their fire died, leaving the room in the glow of the fire and the sunrise through the walls. And then the world was quiet and sleep rushed to her, yet again. What wonders waited for her in her sleep, this time? What magic would tomorrow bring?

The woman's drowsy voice swept over her neck. "Are you warm now?"

The fishmonger's daughter hummed as she drifted to sleep, her answer lost to her slumber.

SHE DREAMED OF A SNARLING WHITE BEAST WITH dark eyes and bloody fangs.

She dreamed of its heavy paws, tipped with razor-sharp claws, tearing through soft sheets and feathered headrests.

She dreamed of its weight, muscle and fat, pinning her to the bed and causing her to bleed.

She dreamed of its breath on the back of her neck.

She dreamed of how soft its fur was.

WHEN SHE WOKE, SHE WAS ALONE IN THE BED. THE sun was dipping low in the sky and, as she stretched in the dim light, she marveled at the length of her dreams. She must've slept the entire day, longer than she ever managed to in the small bed at her family's home. Truly, if she would've even attempted to sleep longer than a short night, she'd have woken up with stiff limbs and an aching neck.

But, today, she woke up feeling refreshed for the first time since she was a child. Rested, she thought, as she observed the room with new eyes. The prisms in the walls and the crackling of the fire and the softness of the sheets below her, the world around her still seemed so impossible, especially as she sat against the pillows, the bed cold beside her.

Where had the woman gone? How long had she been away? She didn't know. But she would find out.

She gathered her courage and pushed the lush blankets away from her body. Her feet grew cold as soon as they touched the floor. She reached for her satchel to change into something else, but, instead, she found a new dress and warm underclothes laid out for her, as well as fur-lined house shoes.

She dressed herself eagerly, sighing at the feeling of the fabric on her shivering skin, as she thought about her day. Strange, she thought, to start her day at the end of it. Her stomach rumbled and, suddenly, she realized how long it'd been since she ate. Despite the rich foods of her last meal with her family, she was hungry again.

The woman's words from last night came back to her. The servants, she remembered, would show her around her new home, and maybe that would include the kitchen, as well. Excitement blossomed inside of her at the thought of another meal with bursting fruits and salted meats and filling grains and—

She pushed open the door to the bedroom and, the moment she did, she found herself in a flurry of snowflakes within the halls. As the snow fell around her, she was greeted by a chorus of sweet, small voices singing her name.

"Welcome!" the voices said, coming from no particular direction. No, in fact, quite the opposite. The voices seemed to be coming from everywhere all at once, high in tone but fading in just enough time for the next voice to pick up where the last left off.

The fishmonger's daughter looked all around, but found no servants, no housekeepers, no cleaners. No one at all. But the voices spoke kindly and spoke her name with excitement, so she asked, "Do you know where I can find the kitchen?"

And the voices chimed back, "The kitchen! Yes! We can show you the kitchen! Down the long hallway!"

So she followed the direction, listening to these bell-like voices as they rang out around her. She went down the long hallway, and then down the corridor, and then passed the wide windows, until she found the kitchen. It was a huge space, filled with all of the tasty treasures she had been imagining, but it was the bowl of the vibrant fruits that caught her eye.

She stared, stomach rumbling again, but hesitated.

The voices tinkled, "Go on! Take a citrus! They're for you!"

"Are you certain?" she said, hand hovering over the bowl. "There are so many!"

"For you!" The voices repeated. "For you! Enjoy!"

The skin of the fruit was tender leather and, when she

dug her thumbs in to pull it apart, the juice was fragrant and the smell made her mouth water. The first bite burst across her tongue, flavorful and perfect and she closed her eyes as she savored the flavor.

"Take a summer berry, too!" the voices encouraged. "They're so sweet! For you!"

Maybe this place would not be so terrible, so terrifying—

A loud noise interrupted her, so loud and animalistic that the orange fell straight from her hands onto the white tile floor when she startled. The voices sounded off too, worried little expressions singing all around her, but gave her no answers as she stepped around her fallen orange and back into the hall with the wide windows.

Outside, the wonderland of the winter waited for the next wanderer to break through the perfect slopes, the sun painting the whole thing in magnificent shades of sunset, as spectacular as orange peel against white tile. It was a tranquil scene, except for the monstrous creature in the middle of it all.

The icebear stalked across the landscape, fur as white as the snow but mouth filled with icicle sharp teeth. It was the size of ski hills, its back the length of her village and its paws wide enough to crush her home between its massive claws. The sun shone off the bright white of its fur, capturing the image of the sky in its reflection.

The fishmonger's daughter gasped as the icebear seemed to look straight at her, gaze catching her face from across the wide, white distance. Its head tilted, as if it could actually see her horror from the snow-covered, sloping hills. Her hands went to her throat, stepping back from the window and running back to the room.

She threw herself on the bed, covering herself with the

thick blanket and burying herself in the downy pillows. Her teeth chattered and her toes grew cold, but she would not leave the comfort of the bed. No, she had been safe there, even when the woman had urged her inside from the blizzard, from the terrible creatures prowling outside. The woman—

The fishmonger's daughter sat up in bed, dread settling inside her.

Where was the woman? Was she safe? Oh, the red of the bear's mouth dyed red with blood— was she safe?

She didn't know. But she would wait. The sun took its time to descend completely but, before long, the sound of heavy footsteps echoed in the hall. The fishmonger's daughter stayed in the bed, still wrapped tightly in the fabrics, until the bedroom door creaked open.

The woman was dressed in the same thick clothes from the night before, but there was a softer expression on her face now, relaxed in a way that she hadn't been. But worry poured through her, and, before she had even considered moving, she launched herself into the woman's arms.

"Are you well?" she asked the woman, cheek pressed to her shoulder. The woman was cold, too cold. Stars above, the woman's skin was freezing. The fishmonger's daughter pulled back, taking stock of her. Her cheeks were ruddy but her lips were not blue. Still, she cupped her face in her own thin hands. "You are cold."

The woman's surprise slowed her answer, but, soon enough, her hands rested over the fishmonger's daughter on her own face. "I am well," she said, voice soothing. The fishmonger's daughter's shoulders sagged in relief. The woman continued, "But I am cold."

"Tell me you did not go outside," she begged. "There was a monster, a bear the size of the sky with sharp teeth and—" She shook as she remembered the image it had made, and her next breath shuddered. She clutched at the woman's cloak. "Tell me you did not. I beg of you."

The woman stared at her for a long moment.

"I cannot," she answered eventually. "For I do not wish to lie to you, sweet girl. But I am safe."

"It is dangerous out there!" she cried, shaking her head.

"Come," the woman said, then, sitting on the bed and urging her into strong arms. The fishmonger's daughter let herself be led, worry melting as the woman pulled her close. The woman touched her cheek, sighing at the warmth of the younger woman's skin, and her words were slow, "I will not tell you to stop your worry, dear one, for I think it would discourage your very nature." The woman's light laugh brushed over her mouth and the fishmonger's daughter licked her lips. The woman's voice deepened, adding, "But you have nothing to fear from the icebear, I promise you."

"But," she returned, shivering at the memory. "It was so big and scary and just outside your home!"

"Oh, darling girl," the woman soothed, eyes kind. "This is its home, too."

The fishmonger's daughter shook her head. "I do not understand."

The woman hummed, as if considering that for the first time. "The icebear," she began slowly, testing her own words, "is a guardian of these lands of ice and cold. In the day, it travels across these strange and wondrous landscapes, providing safe travels to all and greeting its kin throughout the seasonal travels."

The fishmonger's daughter swallowed heavily, eyes flickering to the door. What if it got in?

She whispered, "Does it know I am here?"

The woman's eyes sparkled, voice conspiratorial. "It invited you here."

"Why?" the fishmonger's daughter asked, gasping the word. She clung to the front of the woman's cloak, the white fur soft against her palms. "Please, I am grateful for your kindness. You have saved my family. But, please," she repeated, softer, softer. "Tell me. Why am I here? Where am I? Why me?"

The woman looked at her, then. Truly looked, eyes roaming over brown eyes and sloping nose and curved lips and a smattering of moles. Whatever the woman saw, it made her swallow and nod, as if coming to a decision.

"It is late and it is cold," the woman said gently. The fishmonger's daughter frowned, opening her mouth to plead, but the woman continued, "Join me under the quilts and I will call for supper. Once we are fed and full," she hesitated for only a moment. "I will tell you everything."

She could sense no lie in these words, so she nodded her assent. The woman pulled up the quilt and the warm sheets, and the fishmonger's daughter crawled between them. But before the woman joined, she opened the door and spoke softly into the hall. The fishmonger's daughter heard no response but the woman nodded and shut the door, anyway, before returning to the bed.

Her weight was somehow already familiar to her, as the woman joined her in the warmth of the blankets. She did not hesitate to reach for her and the woman's sigh perfumed their shared space as she was pulled into the embrace. Their bodies pressed together, fingers and toes had just begun to thaw when there was a knock at the door.

She startled, imagining the great icebear at the door with its teeth and paws, but the woman extracted herself from her arms, answering her expression with, "The food."

When she opened the door again, there was no bear or person, servant or otherwise, on the other side. No, instead, a platter of food waited for them.

Her stomach grumbled. The food sent steam spiraling toward the ceiling. The woman set the platter on the bed, beckoning the girl closer. "Come," she said again, holding up a slice of warm bread and spreading it with something sweet smelling and sticky. "Eat, and I will tell you what you wish to know."

The fishmonger's daughter took the bread and nibbled on the end. Her eyes fluttered shut. It was rich and soft, the flavors soothing her shivering and rumbling as it settled in her stomach. When she opened her eyes, the woman was watching her again, amusement crinkling her eyes.

"Good?" the woman asked, mouth twitching upward.

She swallowed, cheeks flushing. "Very."

The woman licked her lips, eyes on her mouth. "Good."

She cleared her throat, raising the bread to her mouth again. "My questions?"

The woman's eyes lost their spark and she nodded, sitting back against the pillows.

"I knew your father."

The bread turned to crumbs in her mouth. Grief stole the taste. She swallowed. "You did?"

"Your father," the woman said, voice gentle with its painful words. "Was a companion of mine, on his vast travels." The woman reached out to clasp the girl's hand in her own. "He was a good man. He told me stories. He often looked to me for direction, and, as much as I could, I looked out for him."

The fishmonger's daughter looked away. "He never mentioned you. I'm sorry."

"Perhaps," she allowed. "He often spoke of you, you know. His daughter, so kind and warm to all. How you helped your mother without being asked. How brightly you smiled when he returned home from a long day on the great salt lakes."

"He did?" she asked, voice cracking.

The woman nodded carefully. "As he died, he asked that I look after you."

"Oh," she answered. "And this is why you have brought me here?"

But the woman shook her head. "No. I was determined to watch over you from afar. And then..."

The woman trailed off. Her face was pink, too, now.

"And then?" the fishmonger's daughter prompted, squeezing her hand.

"And then," the woman finished, their eyes meeting. "You spoke to the stars." She cupped the fishmonger's daughter's cheek, following the bone with her fingers. She swallowed, eyes staying on hers. "You asked if they were warm."

Her next breath stuttered. Her words had been lost to the sky, the question unheard by other ears and unanswered by other mouths. She was alone. Cold and grieving and staring at the lights in the dark above.

"How do you know that?" she gasped.

The woman leaned closer, then, gaze searching her own. Finally, finally, she answered. "Because, sweet girl, when you speak to the stars, sometimes they listen."

She opened her mouth to respond. To ask more questions, to have the woman explain, but she thought about that night. Her back against the snow, the constellations twinkling above her. She thought about their stories, the ones that lulled her to sleep when she, herself, was just a babe and her father smelled of salt and sea.

She recalled the shapes of their cosmic designs, the winking of their eyes and their legends and meanings. The Hunter and his tragic death. The Ram and its fierce protection. The Harp and its golden strings. The Dragon and its glimmering hoard.

And her own favorite, as wide and white as the winter, the Great Bear.

"The icebear," she said, her voice shaking. "The one outside..."

"The journey to the sky was long," the woman answered kindly. "And you slept soundly."

Her throat hurt from all the questions that begged to claw out.

"The castles," she said, voice cracking. "The palaces, the lakes and meadows, the creatures—"

The woman nodded. "All creatures of the cosmos. They were curious. It is not often a human comes to stay." Her voice lowered. "They often visit only just once, when they are neither living nor quite dead."

"Am I dead?" the fishmonger's daughter asked, eyes welling with sadness. She was young. She wanted to live.

"No," the woman answered. "No, you are just my guest here."

"And I'll be able to go home in the spring?"

Something flashed over the woman's handsome face. "If that is what you want."

She sat back, satisfied with those answers. Alive. Free to leave.

Her eyes went to the wide window, the never-ending space of the great snow outside. But the fire was roaring and the quilts were heavy and the bread filled her gut.

The stars, she thought, were better hosts than her own family.

"The icebear," she added softly, causing the woman to look up and meet her eyes. She cleared her throat, speaking a little louder. "You say it protects these lands. That it stays outside for the day, only comes in during the night."

The woman nodded, curiosity in her eyes. "So it does."

The fishmonger's daughter frowned, eyes going back to the swirling blizzards.

"Do you think it is cold?" she wondered, mouth pulling down. "Even such a creature must want to be warm."

There was no response. Not for a long moment, enough time passing that she looked back over at the woman. Those colorless eyes stared at her. Rainbows swirled in them, just as the prisms danced in the ice blocks of the walls, and something impossibly fond filled her expression.

"Yes," the woman said eventually. "Yes, I think the icebear is cold. Has been, for a long time."

"Do you think it wants to come in?" she asked. "Where it is warm?"

A laugh escaped the woman, sounding wet and surprised. She reached out to pull the other closer. The fishmonger's daughter went willingly, letting herself be set in the woman's lap. She fit there, so well, and her arms looped around the woman's next to hold herself even closer.

The woman pressed her forehead to her collarbone, and the fishmonger's daughter held her there.

Her words were muffled, but the woman spoke. "Yes. She wants to come into the warmth. Always."

Pressing a kiss to the woman's head, the fishmonger's daughter considered that. Would it be so terrible, she thought, to share this castle with the creature? Would she mind the monster if it moved inside? Now that she knew more about it, it did not seem so terrible at all, only cold and lonely. She could understand that, more than anyone.

"It is welcome," she said to the woman, then, just as softly. "To share the warmth we have here."

The woman looked up, eyes swimming now, tears at the corners. "Truly? You would welcome a monster into your home?" Her gaze flickered to the room, the fire and the quilts and, finally, to the bed. "To your bed?"

The fishmonger's daughter swallowed but nodded. "If it is cold, let it in."

It was quiet, then, as their eyes met for several breaths. The woman's hand found her face, fingertips rough but touch as light as the snow fall. She moved slowly, then, leaning forward only slightly, and their lips brushed.

A gasp and, then, warmth exchanged with soft presses of their mouths. No heat, not like she was expecting. Only warmth, as steady as glowing coals and soft as butter across bread and sweet as red berries in her mouth.

The woman pulled back. "I will tell her." She swallowed. "That she is welcome."

The fishmonger's daughter nodded, swaying with the feelings in her head. She hummed, eyes heavy, then.

"Sleep now, sweet girl," the woman murmured, kissing her one more time. "And I will let the icebear in."

"Hurry back," she said, already lost to slumber. "It is cold without you."

Even in sleep, she could feel the woman come back to the bed, much later.

Her weight, so familiar now. Her breathing, a steady rhythm. Her arms, strong as they wrapped around her and pulled her close.

The fur of her cloak, lush and prickling against her skin, keeping them both warm.

A kiss to the back of her neck, not yet familiar, but soon would be.

"Tell me," the icebear whispered to the fishmonger's daughter. "Are you warm enough now?"

And, finally, she was.

TRUE LOVE BLOOMS EVERGREEN

BY HELENA V PARIS

True Love Blooms Evergreen

In the bleak mid-winter, an eerie silence had descended upon the nemeton.

Enshrouded in cold and darkness, nary a sound could be heard across the sacred grove. No rustling birds, nor skurrying creatures, not even the howling gusts of wind, which normally blew through the trees with a loud timbre.

The frosty gales had gone utterly still, the branches no longer creaking and moaning in protest of being laden with snow and ice. And, upon a cursory glance, the grim nemeton appeared to be dead.

'You cannot hide from us, Hedera!' Sinister laughter pierced the thick grove, the raucous voices carrying through the trees. 'Reveal yourself!'

A densely shaded thicket had formed near the nemeton's edge, deadfall littering the ground in a tangled heap of fallen trees and branches. Twining vines of ivy climbed up a tall, snowy holm oak tree in a spiral, its leaves a glossy green and its berries as black as night.

It was from these vines that a pair of black eyes opened amidst the leaves. A head soon emerged, followed by spindly arms and legs, and the Ivy Maiden stepped out of her vines as though she had strode out of a dimensional door. Slight and willowy, she donned a short, black tunic and an ivy leaf wreath upon the raven hair that cascaded down her back and cast shadows upon her snow-like skin. Hedera was her name, and she was the first in the thick grove to brave venturing out of her greenery, the others remaining safely in hiding until winter had passed.

Panicked breaths escaped Hedera as the laughter continued to surround her, teasing and taunting her whilst her mind raced with fear. Her kind might have been divinely blessed with long life, but her heart beat fast with such an intensity that it strained to function, like it was on the verge of leaping out of her chest entirely.

Thump! ... Thump! ... Thump! Her chest rose and fell rapidly as her heart continued to thunder from deep within, the sound reverberating so loudly in Hedera's ears that she feared her hunters heard it, too.

Squinting through the snowfall, she peered into the remnants of what was once a bright and flourishing wildwood. A shower of sleet and snow fell with fervent ferocity from the night sky and laid thickly upon the ground, its accumulation piling higher with each passing moment and burying what little foliage still survived underneath. Hedera bore the frost, so bitterly cold that her breath became visible in the winter storm, like a ghostly mist dancing in the air.

Much of the wildlife – bears, hedgehogs and dormice alike – had fallen aslumber months ago, hibernating in the hopes that when they awoke, the harshness of this long winter would all be over.

But they were not the only ones who sought refuge from the chill. The non-migratory birds hid away in their nests, the squirrels in their dreys, the rabbits in their burrows, the deer in the snow on the south-facing slopes.

As it happened, the only creatures who still stirred in the woodland were the sídhe draoí, the faery guardians of the grove. The same guardians who sounded the carnyx through the trees, its intimidating and fear-inducing echoes piercing the silence.

Frozen in place so as to not betray her position, Hedera's eyes scanned the treescape for any sudden movement – a pine needle fluttering down from a branch, an acorn rolling out from underneath a bush, but not a sight was discernible in the dark shadows.

She curled a lock of black hair behind one ear and shut her eyes to concentrate on detecting any sounds, but in the entirety of the nemeton, all she could hear was the sound of her own shallow breathing.

Those who had blown the carnyx were as well hidden as she was.

The Holly King's hunting horn blew once more as the sídhe draoí at his command drew nearer – then again until it was thrice-blown, signalling that a hunt had begun on the eve of Alban Arthan. Meaning the 'Light of the Bear' – it was the time during which the North Star, the tail of the Little Bear constellation, shone brightest upon the nemeton. Dawn would soon bring not only a new day, but the winter solstice – the year's shortest day and the longest night.

'You can run and you can hide ... But there's no escaping us, Hedera. We *will* find you.'

Each and every one of the nemoral creatures that dwelt in the grove knew the Holly King's spies were everywhere: amongst the trees rooted into the earth and the birds flying high in the air. The sídhe draoí in the trees remained perfectly still – always watching, always listening and carrying the secrets they heard upon their leaves as they flew through the breeze.

Not that any breeze still stirred anyway.

Hedera glanced left and right, her chest tightening with apprehension. But she knew better than to hope for a rescue from any of her fellow sídhe draoí. From the deciduous faeries to the evergreens, she had always been misjudged as being cold, dark and quite sinister. They never could trust her climbing vines, which seemed to defy death itself. Not only could her ivy thrive where other trees could not and block out the sunlight most trees needed in order to flourish, but even if her vines were viciously cut away, they somehow managed to return with a vengeance still.

And to them, that made her simply unnatural.

Hedera's eyes flicked to the left again before she placed a tentative, dainty foot forwards upon the blanket of snow. Only for a cold shiver to run down her spine.

'Come out, come out wherever you are ...' echoed a voice that sounded much too close for comfort.

They had found her.

Many of her kind had already lost their lives to the Holly King's endless winter. Each day of the waxing year since his rise to power had been cold and dull, the nemeton's inhabitants held prisoner in a realm of frigid snow and ice. The springs' waters were frozen, food was scarce, and the sídhe draoí were not quite so lucky as the bears – meekly sequestering themselves away in hibernation was not an option.

And yet, despite their distrust of her, Hedera would sooner die before she permitted the Holly King to claim the lives of anyone else. Due mostly in part to her persevering ivy, she alone had a semblance of immortality, which made her the one most likely to survive his merciless wrath. She had a plan, in which the *hunted* would become the *hunter*, and she would defeat him.

If only she could make it there alive.

Selecting a direction at random, Hedera set off at a run. Had she not been one of the sídhe draoí, innately swift and agile, sinking into the snow mounds would have been unavoidable in her flimsy slippers. Rather, she darted through the thicket, zigzagging across the grove in the hopes that an unpredictable course of bends and turns would make it increasingly difficult for them to catch her.

Alas, the hem of her tunic caught on a branch of needles – fir or pine, she was uncertain – as she dashed past. Hedera swept a branch out of the way in her efforts to clear the path ahead and the sharp needles drew blood on her arm. It was an act she instantly recognised to be a careless error on her part as the metallic scent of her blood permeated the air. They could now hunt her with ease.

'Hedera ...' came that unsettling laughter again. 'We can smell you.'

She spun in a circle, trying to locate even one of the voices, and as she turned, she nearly collided into the Fir Lord, one of the Holly King's most ardent conifer followers.

'Boo!' He laughed, delighted at the evident terror upon her face. 'I've got you now.' Broad and stocky in stature, a menacing grin brightened his plain, brown features.

'No, you most certainly do *not*,' she said, steeling herself. Recognising his relaxed demeanour, Hedera seized her opportunity to race past him so quickly that she left nothing but a blur in her wake. She breathed a sigh of relief as she succeeded in evading him, the sounds of him chasing after her through the trees having tapered off after a few moments.

She continued to tap into her enhanced speed, sprinting faster and faster, before she skidded to a stop. The Spruce Lord stood directly in her path, just waiting for her to barrel into him. The faery leant against a tree trunk, his skin so cold and white that it was tinged with blue. But after she took in his frail appearance, Hedera heeded him no mind and continued on her way into the heart of the nemeton.

To her astonishment, he did not seem inclined to pursue her.

In the biting chill, Hedera's movements began to slow and her breathing grew laboured. Even the heighteneded speed of the sídhe draoí had its limits.

Her legs finally gave out, buckling beneath her and refusing to go any further, when a large, calloused hand encircled her wrist to drag her to her feet and hold her in place. Had she not felt his tight grasp for herself, she might have sworn the black skin of her captor was merely that of a dark shadow. However, the fearsome Pine Lord loomed over her, staring down at her with narrowed eyes.

'Going somewhere?' he sneered.

Unwilling to be intimidated by him, she defiantly raised her head and met his eyes. 'Yes,' Hedera said. 'Away from you.' She pulled away from him, struggling to escape his clutches, the sensation of his bony fingers so painful that they were as sharp as pine needles digging into her skin.

'And yet, here you stand.'

'Not ... for ... much ... longer!' Frustrated, she thrashed and flailed against him. Hedera used her free arm to inflict as much damage as possible, scratching and clawing with her fingernails in the hopes of drawing blood, but the Pine Lord remained as immovable as a mighty tree trunk.

Despite her valiant attempts at freeing herself, he did not budge in the slightest.

So Hedera did what any sensible faery maiden would do.

She kneed him in the groin.

In an instant, the Pine Lord crumpled to the ground, his face contorted with agony whilst his hands covered his crotch in desperation.

Hedera resisted the temptation to roll her eyes. She had *barely* touched him.

Faery lords were such babies.

Finally free from his grasp, a fresh surge of adrenaline coursed through Hedera's veins and she continued to flee across the grove, leaving him to voice his livid groans and curses into the empty, uncaring air. Since the Pine Lord had made it abundantly clear that he cared not for the fate that would befall her once he delivered her to the Holly King, why would she be foolish enough to grant a moment's thought to his well-being?

'Well, that wasn't very sporting of you,' emerged the voice Hedera dreaded most of all. Low and cruel in tone, it sliced into the soundless void like a knife. 'Don't you know you could seriously injure a faery lord that way?'

Hedera froze in place, a creeping chill running down her spine like spiders down a vine. 'He'll live,' she said, her breath caught in her throat. Excruciatingly slowly, she turned, a ring forming around her scantily-clad feet in the snow.

Ilex, the Holly King himself. He stood with an air of haughty elegance about him. Tall and pale, he regarded her with an uncharacteristically amused expression through his white lashes. Ornamented with ripened berries as red as blood and pointed leaves as sharp as thorns, his holly wreath crown was a pop of colour against his long, white hair, the strands so bright they appeared to be woven by starlight. It shone against the thick, red winter coat he wore – which was albeit more white than red in the heavy snowfall.

Ilex drew closer to Hedera as he gripped the holly branch staff he wielded, his black boots crunching in the snow. Trapped in place, Hedera was ensnared in his path.

Ilex didn't walk, he stalked towards his prey, a palpable coldness emanating from him whilst he did. After all, he was the Rigonemetis – the King of the Sacred Grove – and he relished the season in which his terrifying power was at its pinnacle. It took little effort on his part to instil his subjects with paralysing fear.

A fear Hedera would be certain to resist every step of the way.

'If it isn't the Ivy Maiden,' he said, a soft laugh escaping his lips. 'You've been driving my lords mad, having them chase you around the nemeton for months.'

'*I* did nothing,' Hedera replied through gritted teeth. 'I've asked you – repeatedly – to leave me alone.'

He shook his head in disbelief with a humourless chuckle. 'I offered you a crown, to make you my winter queen, and yet, you ran after my proposal. Why?'

She cast her eyes downwards to avoid the piercing gaze of his ice blue eyes, her stomach clenched with nerves. 'Because my heart already belongs to another.'

'He's dead,' Ilex said, a puzzled look crossing his face. 'He's *been dead* for half a year.' He spat out the words as though death should have been enough to stop Hedera from loving him. 'I rule the winter, and you – the Ivy Maiden – were born in the dark and cold of my domain.

We're connected, you and I. And, quite frankly, I'm a much better match for you than he ever was.'

'That doesn't matter. Not to me. I'm sorry, but I cannot marry you.'

'Yes, you can. You're simply choosing not to.'

A robin abruptly interjected into their conversation to sing through the trees – the storm-cloud bird – whose unnerving melody ominously indicated a storm was on its way.

Several thoughts at once rapidly churned through Hedera's mind as she considered how best to convince Ilex to let her go. Her plans to defeat him did not consist of marriage.

'Please, Your Majesty, I'm not worthy of being your queen. Can't you see there's nothing special about me? Our own kind does their best to avoid me. There are far more desirable faeries in the grove aplenty for you to choose from.'

Ilex closed the space between them, his jaw set with such frustration that his angular features sharpened, making them appear to have been carved from ice. 'I've chosen *you* to marry, Hedera, and I am your king. You cannot deny me. I will have you for my wife, even if I have to drag you all the way back to my palace in order to claim you.'

Alarmed by his brazenness, she stepped backwards from him, her foot snapping a fragile twig that laid upon the thick snow. And suddenly, the very earth itself opened up before her.

A massive gorge sprang into being, which led down to the pitch-black depths of the realm of the dead. Snow and rocks tumbled down the edge as she drew closer, stepping hesitantly towards it. Had death come for Hedera? Was she to finally re-join her love in the afterlife?

Slowly, a thick, outstretched arm reached up from the blackness, kissed by the sun and corded with muscles. 'I don't suppose you could help me up, would you?'

She *knew* that voice. It was the one she thought she would never hear again.

'Quercus?' Hedera asked breathlessly and rushed forwards. She grasped his hand and, with great difficulty, used all of her augmented strength to heave him over the gorge's edge as he collapsed with a soft thump upon the snow. In a state of complete and utter incredulity, Hedera stared down at him, her chest quickly rising and falling as her breathing slowly steadied from the exertion of the task.

The faery on the ground rose to his feet in one smooth movement, shaking off the snow which had collected upon his green, oak leaf cloak before he re-adjusted the oak branch bow and quiver of arrows hanging on his shoulder. He was tall and muscular, his skin bright and tanned, with a broad smile as radiant as the sun. All browns, greens and other earthly tones, Quercus seemed to be a true descendant of the earth, more so than the other faeries in the grove. A crown of oak leaves and acorns adorned his light brown hair whilst he tilted back his head, deeply inhaling the crisp scent of the nemeton.

The Oak King had returned.

He glanced over to the Holly King, a quiet fury settling over his features. 'Now, let me make myself quite clear: You can kill me. You can steal my throne. But *do not* attempt to seduce my mate.'

'No,' Ilex breathed, his eyes wide and his voice as soft as a whisper. 'I killed you! Back in mid-summer, I slayed you!'

'That you did, brother. Thanks for that, by the way.'

'What's the point of killing my foes if they don't *remain dead*?' he crossly muttered to himself. 'We're not finished, you and I. This fight isn't over.' With that, Ilex quickly retreated into the distance, where a large wooden sleigh awaited him in the trees, the wood stained red from the juice of holly berries. It was drawn by eight stags and steered by the Yew Lord, a hunched and creepy faery with beady eyes, whose yew trees were known as the trees of death due to their poisonous berries. Cunning and manipulative, he was the one who had orchestrated Ilex's quest for power. He slithered around the grove in his hooded robes, whispering venomous and traitorous thoughts into the Holly King's ears.

The sound of twinkling bells indicated the sleigh's departure, tufts of snow kicking up behind it, after which Quercus turned to face Hedera with a smile from ear-to-ear. He dropped his bow and quiver to the ground before he spread his arms wide, eagerly beckoning to her.

Without a moment's hesitation, she leapt and hooked her arms around his neck, burying her face into his broad shoulders as she savoured his return. His thick, strong arms came around to envelope Hedera in a warm embrace, like a ray of sunshine washing over her.

At long last, they had been reunited. She had experienced no joy since the waning year, when Quercus still lived and reigned as the Rigonemetis. How she had missed his earthy scent, his protective arms, his gentle touch. He was her home. *This* was the faery she had willingly given her heart to, from long before until forevermore.

A deep – perhaps even spiteful – sense of satisfaction settled over Hedera, since she knew theirs was the truest form of love Ilex could never hope to know. He deserved to experience solely loneliness and misery after all he put them through during these dark months. Despite his age and wisdom, it was rather strange the Holly King had never learnt that desolation and cruelty did little to win someone's heart. Love could not be forced, it was as natural as breathing. All one could do was let it happen as the gods willed it, and cherish it for as long as it lasted.

Out of the corner of her eye, surprisingly awake, rabbits appeared beneath the bushes, the small, furry creatures softly hopping in the snow.

'But how?' Hedera asked, pulling away from Quercus after a few precious moments. 'How are you alive? I saw what Ilex had done to your major oak, cutting into it and dripping poisonous holly berry juice upon the cuts before leaving it to decay. None of the sídhe draoí could have possibly survived that.'

It was afterwards that the greenwood had turned white, the land becoming infertile as the plant life commenced to wither away into nothing.

'I'm not certain,' he responded. 'Although, I presume my mother would know.'

'I was actually hoping to locate her when Ilex cornered me here. Might you know where she is? I know she dwells in the heart of the nemeton, but where exactly?' Now that Ilex had returned, an entirely different plan had formed in her mind.

'Come. I'll show you.' Quercus reached down to retrieve his bow and quiver, offering a hand to Hedera, and when she placed her small hand into his rather large and calloused one, they sped through the trees together in a blur.

Moments later, they arrived at a haunted clearing in the grove where a mighty oak, ash and hawthorn stood together

– the trees most hallowed to the sídhe draoí – all of which were dead in this harsh winter.

The oak was in particularly dire shape due to the Holly King's sabotage, the rank smell of woodrot and decay hanging in the air, but the spring of healing waters underneath already had small cracks beginning to appear in the ice. All that was frozen starting to melt once Quercus stepped foot into the realm of the living. He was akin to a breathing sun, shining his brightness and warmth upon the nemeton.

'By the goddess,' Hedera said as she took in the damage to his oak. 'I can scarcely believe Ilex would do this to another faery, much less his own brother.'

'Mhm,' Quercus grunted noncommittedly. 'With a twin like mine, who needs enemies?'

'Quercus, my Oak of the Sun,' came a soothing, melodic voice from behind them.

Hedera and Quercus swung around in unison as Nemetona entered the clearing, the Mother of the Sacred Grove, without whom the nemeton would not exist. Striding forwards, she moved past them to take her seat upon a modest wooden throne at the centre of the three withered trees. A regal sceptre that reflected moonlight was clasped in her hand whilst three hooded spirits stood guard behind her and an enormous ram took its position at her feet. Nemetona had an ethereal beauty and grace to her, greatly resembling Quercus with her dark hair and sun-kissed skin.

'How lovely to see you. Tell me, what brings you to my share of the grove?' she asked.

'Hello, mother. We're actually here on behalf of my mate. It appears she has something to ask of you,' Quercus responded, gesturing to Hedera at his left.

Nemetona's eyes shone like stars as she appraisingly regarded Hedera. 'The Ivy Maiden. I've heard ample about you.'

All good things, Hedera could not help but hope. 'Great goddess,' Hedera said, deferentially bowing her head. 'Ever since Ilex seized the crown, the nemeton has spiralled into darkness, an endless winter. We're all suffering from starvation. If not for Quercus' acorns, which we ground down to make bread in replacement of grain, the few of us who remain probably wouldn't have survived these past few months.'

'I'm sorry to hear that, but what would you ask of me?'

'Quercus has now ... *somehow* ... returned. Can you not replace Ilex with him as king, seeing the crown was his in the first place?'

'I'm afraid it doesn't work like that. Are you aware of who my consort is, child?'

Hedera nodded. 'Leucetius, the Light-Bringer in the heavens.'

'Correct. He is the god of lightning, thunder, storms and, most importantly, *war*. It was his decree that the title of Rigonemetis can only be won in battle by challenging and killing the current king. The victor wins the crown.'

'But Ilex never formally challenged me,' Quercus said. 'He employed poison and trickery in order to weaken me before killing me.'

'I suppose, technically, your father never laid out any rules forbidding that. So long as a life is sacrificed – blood must be spilt to ensure the arrival of the next season – it's of little consequence if both parties are knowing participants.'

'How is Quercus even alive?' Hedera asked. 'Ilex killed him. Not that I'm complaining,' she quickly added.

'You of all the sídhe draoí, with your thriving ivy,

should know nothing in nature ever truly dies. Everything returns to the earth and lives again in some form or another. Now, as for Ilex and Quercus? My evergreen twins are two halves of a whole. Without one, the other would cease to exist. Sadly, I'm afraid that – thanks to their father – they're both trapped in an eternal, seasonal battle for supremacy. A battle which will only end with the demise of the nemeton.'

'So there's nothing we can do?' Hedera asked, dejected. She had placed all her dreams and wishes upon Nemetona being able to aid them in the Holly King's defeat.

'Of course, there is. Quercus can challenge Ilex himself and win. Although, I should hope you shan't stoop to Ilex's level and resort to poison. I raised the both of you to conduct yourselves with gallantry and honour.'

Quercus glanced over at his mother. 'I'm not quite certain Ilex took those lessons to heart.'

'You, Quercus, are the strong protector and your elder brother, the courageous warrior, of the nemeton. For different reasons, you're both worthy of wearing the crown. I'm certain you'll be able to defeat him, should you set your mind to it.'

'But it's mid-winter,' Hedera said. 'Ilex's power is now at its peak, making him impossible to subdue through normal means.'

Nemetona heaved a sigh, looking between Hedera and Quercus. 'I suppose you're right. Well, seeing that Ilex had the advantage last time, it seems only fair that you should be given a boon, too.' She arose from her throne and stepped over the ram, gliding towards the snags. She approached the hawthorn – the most prominent of the faery trees – and collected a branch of deadwood. It rose from her palm into the air, parts of it shaving off to shape an arrow shaft. Then, she broke off a small pointed part of her sceptre and attached it to the shaft's end to form the arrowhead.

Hedera and Quercus moved to join her, and Nemetona presented Quercus with the divinely-crafted arrow. 'With this arrow, you cannot miss your target, but you may only shoot it once. So use it wisely.'

Gazing at it, Quercus turned it over in his palm. The arrow twinkled in the moonlight, as though it was sprinkled with stardust.

'Thank you, goddess,' Hedera said, her tone reverent. She gently touched the arrow with her finger.

'And you, Hedera,' said Nemetona. 'You must remember one thing: The fate of the nemeton may reside in my sons' hands, but you ... you're the key.'

'The key?' She shook her head in confusion. 'The key to what?'

'That, I'm afraid, you must discover for yourself.'

'But that doesn't tell me anything!' she exclaimed.

'Many mysteries lie within this grove, but I often find that wisdom exists all around you, if only you care to listen. Best of luck, my dear.' And with that, she simply vanished out of sight, as though she had never been there at all.

What could her words have possibly meant?

'Wait!' Hedera shouted after her, but it was no use. As was common practice with the gods, their divine wisdom was often bestowed in the form of cryptic riddles, most of which made little sense. Exasperated, she gently nudged Quercus in his side. 'So what's the plan?'

'It's quite simple really. The plan is war.'

Quercus spent the next few minutes pacing in circles around the clearing. His mother's boon was already nocked in his bow, ready to be shot at a moment's notice. 'Ilex, you coward!' Quercus bellowed, his shouts resounding through the trees as he sought to attract his brother's attention. 'Come out and face me! Isn't this what you wanted?! Well, here I stand, waiting for you!'

Ilex materialised a moment later whilst a flash of lightning struck the ground, a trick he had learnt from their father. 'Ready for round two, are we?' He lazily smirked, but he was unprepared when Quercus shot him straight in the chest with the arrow in the blink of an eye.

Ilex roared in anger as gleaming red blood gushed from the wound. He transformed himself into a wren, its brown feathers the result of being scorched by Quercus' sun in their youth, and took to the sky.

Determined to avenge his own death, Quercus shifted into a white-breasted robin and followed him, as well.

Unfortunately for Hedera, she was left behind and filled with worry as she feared losing Quercus a second time. She could not endure it again and, furthermore, she *would not*. If he died, then so would she. They were two notes in the same song, two steps in the same dance, and they would remain together as one, regardless if that meant in the realm of the living or the dead.

Her gaze trailed skywards, locked on the birds engaged in a violent skirmish, and she was not alone. The rustling of branches alerted her to the presence of numerous flocks of wren songbirds and white-breasted robins perched in the trees, a rapt audience for their masters.

Wings, claws and beaks, the brothers used any body part they could to inflict damage upon each other. A swipe of a wing from one, a slash of a claw from the other. Ilex lunged directly for Quercus' neck, nearly nipping him with his beak, but Quercus deftly dove out of the way.

He descended back down upon the ground and returned to his faery form, slowly pacing around the clearing with his arms wide to narrate the ongoing spectacle to their onlookers. Ilex might have been their king, but it was Quercus who commanded the nemeton's attention. Trees shook out their snowy leaves, animals drew closer and faeries Hedera had not caught sight of in months emerged from the grove in order to get a better view. All of them curious as to who would be king come sunrise.

'Behold your cowardly king!' Quercus hollered, trying to goad Ilex into a response. 'He's quite content to poison his enemies, but when it comes to actual combat, he takes to the skies! Some "courageous warrior," indeed!'

At the nermoral creatures' laughter, Ilex joined his brother upon the frost-kissed ground. He raised his palm, shooting shards of ice at Quercus. 'How's that for a coward?' he scoffed.

Quercus ducked and summoned the power of a fiery sun in his palm. The flames he expelled melted his brother's ice before it could get anywhere near him.

Back and forth, fire and ice, the brothers appeared evenly matched in skill as they traded blows in earnest, despite Ilex commanding more power during the mid-winter. It was as though Quercus had returned to the realm of the living with newfound strength. Perhaps they did not truly need Nemetona's arrow after all.

This was the battle of two brothers, in which Hedera was not expected to interfere. But at the rate their conflict was going, it appeared as though it would never end. And their hatred of each other ran so deep that the likelihood of them ruling the grove together was slim to none.

Something had to be done if this was to ever be resolved.

You're the key, returned Nemtona's voice in her mind.

The key, the key. Was she meant to engage in this fight after all?

Whether she was or not, Hedera had already decided that she was.

She stepped towards the two brothers, twisting out of harm's way when a volley of icicles launched past her.

'Hedera!' Quercus yelled as he shot a blazing fireball at his brother's head. 'Get out of here! You're going to get yourself hurt!'

Ilex dove aside, landing in the snow, his jaw jutted out with rage. But before he could arise from the ground, someone else did it for him.

Vines of ivy shot out of Hedera's palms, twining tightly around his wrists and ankles to anchor him in place against the oak he had destroyed. A fitting, poetic end for him. He struggled against the ivy, reminding her of her earlier experience with the Pine Lord. 'This is for how you tormented us through the dark months. It's about time they turned clear again,' she said. 'Quercus, now!'

Quercus strode forwards and reached over his shoulder to retrieve an arrow from his quiver. He tightly grasped it in his hand before plunging it deeply into Ilex's neck with as much force as he could muster. Blood sprayed in every direction and splashed onto the flocks of robins' white breasts, transforming the birds into robin redbreasts. The leaves of the holly trees bounding the grove instantly turned yellow and underwent leaf drop, no longer evergreen.

Without moving or even breathing, Quercus stood vigilant as he watched the life quickly ebb out of his brother until he finally breathed a deep sigh of relief.

The Holly King was dead.

At last, the harsh and endless winter was at its end as the earth began to awaken from its slumber. The golden sun broke through the clouds and the crisp air swirled around, high in the sky, with the promise of the coming spring. Animals emerged from hibernation whilst plants and flowers found themselves re-born, pushing up from the soil beneath the melting blanket of snow. Deafening cheers and voices broke out across the nemeton, the sídhe draoí thrilled with the knowledge that brighter days were ahead. Every face shone with a bright smile, each voice laced with laughter. They celebrated and feasted around lit fires, dancing in rings, singing songs and telling stories.

The Holly King was gone, and the Oak King reigned once more. Although, this time, the Ivy Queen was by his side.

'Come with me,' he said, drawing her towards his major oak tree. This, too, had returned to life, a sprig of mistletoe having fallen from the greening oak leaves.

Hedera reached up to pick one of the white berries until Quercus grabbed her hand. 'Don't, they're poisonous.'

'They are? Then, why did you bring me here?' she asked.

'To do this.' He gently took her in his arms and pulled her face to his, his lips soft and tender upon hers. Slowly and desperately, he poured out all of the love that he had for his mate, and Hedera eagerly returned his affections. So much time they had lost during their separation, and they would not waste a moment longer.

In the branches above, a robin redbreast sang once more before it flew away.

'Are you not going to make a wish?' Quercus asked, speaking against her mouth.

'Why would I? All of my wishes have already come true,' Hedera said and continued to pepper him with kisses.

He smiled. 'And dare risk bad luck to befall us? How unwise.'

'All right. Well, how about this?' Hedera paused long enough to gaze into his warm, twinkling brown eyes. 'I wish that we will live happily ... ever ... after.'

Quercus feigned a pondering look before casting a teasing wink her way. 'That sounds to be in order.'

And happily they did live, for the following days, the following weeks, the following months, even as the Holly King laid in wait, patiently anticipating his re-birth come mid-summer.

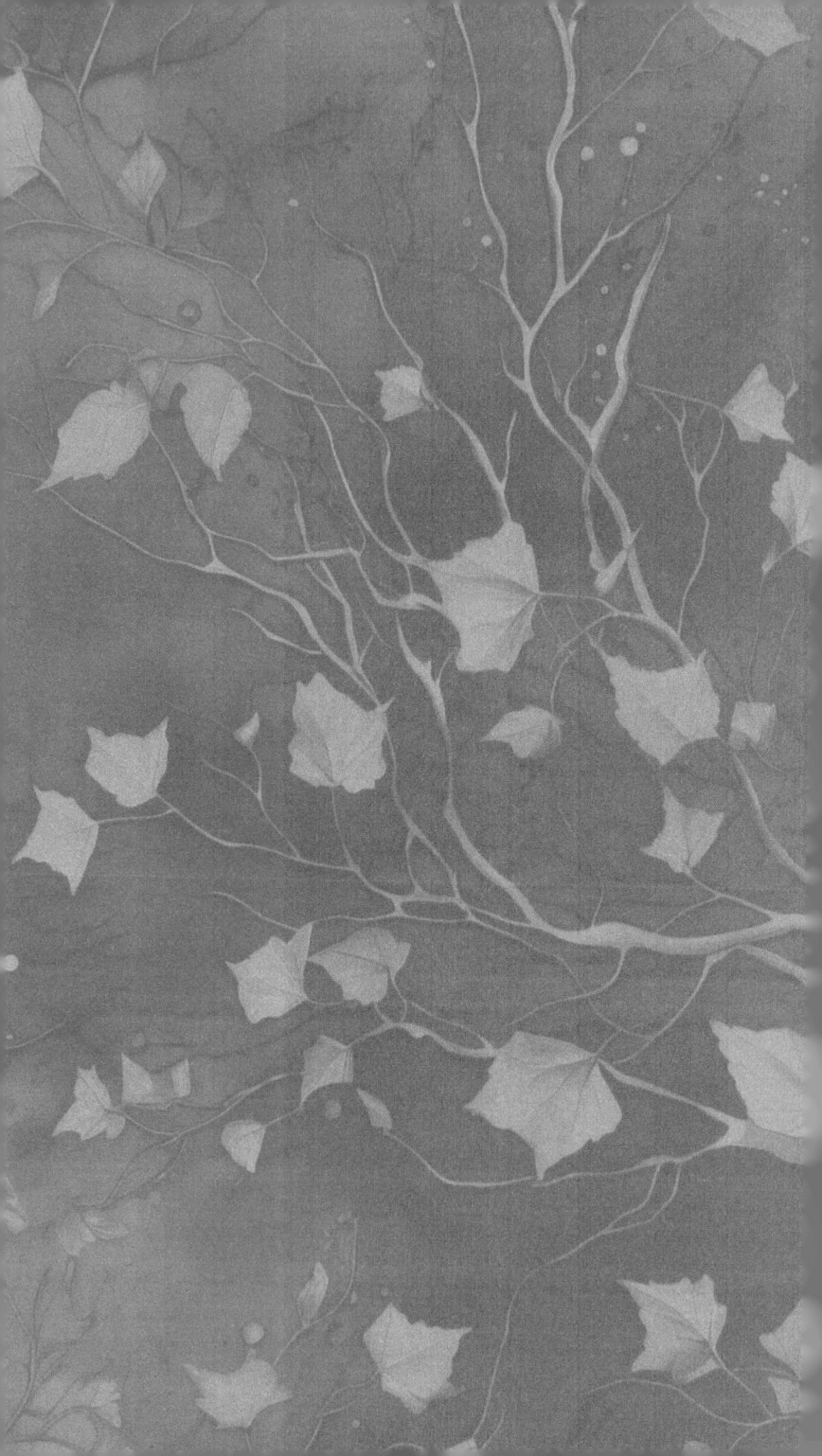

ELEMENTS
OF THE
STONE

BY ANNIE WELCH

Elements of the Stone

BRIAR

My boots crunched in the snow as I chased after my sisters, a flurry of soft powder kicking up behind me. Elsie's mauve skirt floated like a petal above the snow, a glimpse of spring against the monochrome field we ran through.

"Keep up, Briar!" Elsie threw over her shoulder, and I willed my legs to move faster. Mabel huffed out a laugh that danced back to me on the December air, her brown dress and glossy auburn hair making her look like a falling autumn leaf. I finally managed to gain on them as they approached the old wooden gate and were forced to slow. Lungs aching, my hot breath formed clouds in front of my face.

"Why are we *running*?" I managed to gasp out, placing my hands on my knees and doing my best to will away the stitch forming within my ribs. "The tree lighting isn't until sundown!"

"We have to get a good spot," Mabel responded

breathily, walking back towards me and prying my mitten covered hands off of my knees, bringing me up to face her. "The whole village will be in the square tonight."

"And you don't want to get stuck behind grumpy Mr Jones, do you?" Elsie chuckled from where she sat on the gate, swinging her legs impatiently. True. If we were attending the annual tree lighting ceremony, I would like to be able to *see* the tree.

"Perhaps we can compromise with a jog instead of a sprint?"

"Deal." Mabel decided and I nodded before she began pulling me along behind her onto the icy road that led into the heart of the village. The compromise turned out to benefit us all, since even at a light jog the ice was deadly. Elsie was lucky to be caught by Mrs Thorne, out walking her small dog Toby, before she could topple backwards over a short garden wall.

"You girls need to be more careful when the weather is like this," she'd berated and after Elsie offered a swift and grateful thank you, we all jogged off. "*Walk*, little seasons!" she called after us, and we giggled as we held onto each other for support. *Seasons.* She'd called us the village's little seasons for as long as I could remember. Although we all came from the same mother and father, with me as the middle child, we all looked completely different. Like the seasons, Mrs Thorne said. Elsie was all softness and spring dew, with her curly blonde hair, green eyes, and rosy cheeks. Whereas Mabel's glossy red hair and amber eyes made her look like a snapshot of an autumn forest. I was winter, according to Mrs Thorne, with my wild dark hair that reached my hips, grey eyes, and my preference for linens and wools in blacks and blues.

As we approached the village square, I realised my

sisters had been right to hurry. There were already people milling about, vendors had set up stalls selling warm buttered popcorn, and the scent of mulled wine drifted over to us as we crowded in. Mabel pulled three shiny coins from her skirt pocket and dragged us over to the mulled wine stall, getting us all a little cup to keep ourselves warm as we waited for the ceremony to begin. A gorgeous Douglas fir had been taken from the nearby woods and was now standing proudly in the center of the village square, red and gold baubles of varying sizes scattered all over its bushy boughs.

I linked arms with my sisters and we crowded close enough to smell the fresh scent of the tree and admire the ornaments. The wine did the trick, warming my bones, and eventually, the chatter quieted down as Mr Robinson, the village head, approached the front of the tree.

"Welcome all to this year's annual tree lighting ceremony!" His voice boomed out over the small crowd. "Before the lights go on, as usual, please take your neighbour's hand and lend us your voices." It was the same carol every year—my sisters and I knew it by heart and so we started singing in unison with the rest of the village, voices soaring together over the square. As we all sang out the last verse, the tree came alight with a gorgeous warm glow, lighting everyone's faces and the square itself. A cheer went up into the air and me and my sisters found ourselves in a group hug, giggling and being careful not to spill our wine. A few more carols and a performance from the Morris dancers later, most of the village had started to move off down the lane, on their way back home. But Mabel, Elsie and I hovered around an oak table by the hearth fire in one of the small pubs surrounding the square. Another cup of mulled wine was cradled within each of our hands as we watched the tree glowing and a fresh snow start to fall through the window.

Mabel and Elsie were talking amongst themselves about the ribbons or boots they hoped would be gifted to them this year, but I'd faded out of the conversation, quietly watching the snow. My eyes were starting to get heavy when I noticed a shadow move in the lamp light at the edge of the square. I blinked my eyes back into focus, scanning the trees, wondering if it was just tiredness that had my eyes playing tricks on me when I saw the movement again.

My heart thrummed a little faster in my chest and I found myself slowly standing, sliding my now-empty cup away from me. My sisters noticed my movement and halted their conversation. "I think I'm going to head home," I announced, trying to keep my eyes on the square's perimeter without drawing their attention.

"We'll walk with you," Mabel said, about to lift her cup to drain its contents.

"No, no. It's fine." I placed my hand on her wrist, preventing her from gulping down the rest of her drink.

"You two stay here, finish your wine and conversation. I'm just getting tired." I yawned for good measure before pulling my charcoal wool cloak over my shoulders and making for the door before they could stop me. I wasn't sure what I was thinking, going out into the cold alone after a shadow, but there was a familiar pull I couldn't ignore. The shadow moved again and I followed the tug deeper into the trees. As I entered the darkness, twigs snapped beneath my feet and my heart fluttered with adrenaline. For years now, I'd had the feeling of being watched sometimes while I was out in the forests and fields. I'd always chalked it up to an animal, but now... "Hello?" I called out tentatively as I ducked beneath the snowy branches, but the forest was silent and the shadow was nowhere to be seen. As I made to step over a broken branch, my cloak snagged on a blackthorn tree, jolting me back into its sharp branches and the few lonely fruits it still bore despite the lateness of the season. A thorn caught my cheek as I twisted to untangle myself from the tree's icy grasp and I winced but froze when I spotted something glinting in the brush above my head.

A pendant, hanging from a branch on a delicate silver chain. I tugged off one mitten with my teeth and reached out until my bare fingers grazed the cool metal. As they did, I lost sight of the forest around me, my vision no longer my own.

For a flash, I was looking at an old oak tree in broad daylight. The scent of hawthorn still lingered in my nose, at odds with the dark snowy forest that raced back to me when I yanked my fingers away from the pendant.

I steadied myself and took a few deep breaths before gazing curiously up at the necklace again. The pendant itself was an oval frame, and suspended within was a stone unlike anything I'd seen before. Some parts were clear, blueish like a frozen lake but with green swirls of what looked like moss throughout. It was beautiful.

There was something familiar about the oak tree it had shown me. The way the light filtered through its leaves, the scent of the hawthorn... I'd been there before, I was sure of it. But when?

Before I could think it through, I was reaching up again, fingers outstretched to snag the pendant down from where it hung in the blackthorn. As I pulled it free, the snowy forest I stood in once again vanished, replaced with the oak tree and its swaying leaves in the sweet spring air. I took a few small steps towards the oak and gasped when a sharp scratch at my wrist had me dropping the necklace, back again in the snowy woods at the edge of the town square, having just almost walked face first back into the thorny brush.

I contemplated for a moment, staring down at the stone shining in the moonlight and half-obscured by snow, before pulling my mitten back on and tentatively scooping the necklace up, relieved to find the frozen forest around me stayed in place. In the distance, the bells of the inn door chimed, and the unmistakable voices of my sisters faintly carried across the square. I shoved the necklace swiftly into the pocket of my skirts and made a beeline for the lane back towards the house, skidding and sliding on the snow but managing to stay upright. Once I'd sprinted and slipped halfway up the lane, I slowed back to a walking pace, acting as nonchalant as I could. "Briar!" Elsie called out from behind me as the pair entered the lane, and I jumped and spun around as if I'd had no idea they were there. They caught up to me quickly, panting little clouds of hot breath out of their wine-stained mouths. "We couldn't leave you to walk home alone in the cold!" Mabel puffed out, linking her arm around mine as we marched as one the rest of the way home.

I WOKE BEFORE MY SISTERS THE FOLLOWING morning and retrieved the necklace from where I'd hidden it, wrapped in a handkerchief in the false bottom of my bedside drawer. It was the solstice, the shortest day of the year, and the sun still slumbered beneath the horizon as I laced up my boots. With the pendant in my pocket, I snuck carefully out of the kitchen door. I'd tossed and turned all night, thinking about that oak tree, and why I felt it was so familiar.

In the end, I'd decided to wake up early today to make the most of the little light we had and go out in search of the tree. As far as my sisters were concerned, I'd gone out to harvest greenery for the mantle and the dinner table. They wouldn't question it since I often spent time out with my basket foraging in the wilds surrounding the village. As I stepped into the trees behind my house, beyond the fields, I slipped the necklace out of my pocket and tugged off one glove, pressing a determined finger to the stone.

I had been starting to doubt on my way here that I'd seen anything at all last night. Perhaps I'd been overtired and cold with a wine hazy mind but, sure enough, at first contact I lost sight of the winter sky and misty fields around me. I slowly turned in my new environment, trying to take in as many details as possible, searching for some clue as to the direction of the old oak. I heard a river rushing to my left in this spring-kissed snapshot, which I hadn't noticed last night, and that gave me my heading. Fisting the necklace into my still-gloved left hand, I returned to my snowy scene in the present and marched ahead, aiming for the one river I knew rushed like that through these woods.

It wasn't a long walk. It was one we did often growing up, but usually only in the spring and summer when there was enough light to walk there and back and still spend a whole day by the river, splashing in the shallows and basking in the sun to dry our clothes. But it had been four years since we'd spent a summer day by the river. I had been eighteen.

After walking for another half an hour, the sound of the river reached me and before long I was right upon it, turning in circles looking for a hint of that oak in the canopy. I made my way through and past a grove of birch trees, and entered a small clearing, with a mighty oak tree standing proudly in the centre.

THEODORE

I HEARD HER BEFORE I SAW HER. HER DELICATE footsteps crunching through the snow announced her presence and, before I could turn and run, there she was. Bundled in her woolen skirts and cloak with an empty basket over her elbow, her grey-blue eyes scanning curiously over the clearing.

"Hello?" Her gentle voice sang out. She wasn't supposed to be able to see me, but at the town square last night she had definitely seen *something*.

I knew it had been risky to come so close into town, but I had to see her. The way her hair shone in the tree light, the smile spreading over her face as her voice soared over the square with the other village folk.

It warmed my frozen heart in a way that nothing else did.

But I could never engage with her. Elementals had always been forbidden to make contact with the humans that roamed their lands. It was our most absolute rule, drilled into us from childhood all the way up to our eighteenth birthday when we were finally assigned a wilds to care for.

But no one had prepared me for just how enchanting these humans could be.

During my very first spring in this land, four years ago now, I was talking with the old oak tree I called home when

I'd heard the most beautiful peal of laughter, ringing like bells through the trees. I was certain even the old oak itself had relaxed and swayed as the sound rolled over it.

Before I'd even made a conscious decision to move, my legs were carrying me in her direction, mesmerised by the sound, desperate to see the lips it had rang from. The first moment I saw her face my heart shuddered in my chest.

She was up to her knees in the river, her skirts tucked oddly around her waist to keep them dry and her dark, untameable hair was coming loose from its pins in waves and ringlets that framed her face and trailed down her exposed neck.

She looked like a wild thing, and my heart beat so fast it scared me. I'd almost surged forward, dropped to my knees and begged for her name, but instead forced myself to stagger back. I ran for the oak before I could do anything unforgivable, like make myself known and tempt the wrath of the elders for even wanting to do the forbidden.

Panicking, pacing, and clenching my fists in an attempt to control myself, I tried to take the human *need* I felt stirring in my chest, my bones, the very soul of me, and cast it out. But as I unclenched my fist, a small, smooth stone lay there, forged of all that feeling, and I couldn't cast it away. Parts were the same colour as her eyes, a gorgeous chalcedony. Other parts were the same colour as mine, the moss of the forest. And all throughout ran veins of sparkling quartz that looked like snow.

As I beheld her now, standing in the snow and looking like she was crafted by the season itself, my heart shuddered again to be so close to her. Closer than I had been since that first sighting. Clasped in her gloved hand was the pendant I'd worn every day since, until I'd lost it last night in my rush to get away from her.

Despite separating that onslaught of emotion I'd felt that spring into the stone, I'd remained intrigued by the wild girl. I'd watched over her from afar, falling more and more into obsession as I saw the respect she held for the natural land she trod lightly through. *My* land.

We had been taught that humans were a blight on the natural world, taking without care from the very land that sustained them. Greedy, poisonous creatures that would have the earth wither and die for their own selfish desires if left to their own devices. But my sweet wild girl was the opposite of everything I'd ever been warned against. The delicate way she foraged from nature but always left something in return, whether it be wildflower seeds, food for the birds or dishes of water for the deer when the summer peaked was a stark contrast to the image of humans I'd been taught to avoid.

And I could not stay away from her.

I stood hidden behind the mighty oak as a precaution more than anything, since human folk couldn't see us. I'd walked past many men and women out gathering firewood or having a picnic in these woods, and never had a head turned in my direction. It was wildly freeing but painfully lonely.

"Hello?" she called out again and I crouched down, willing my racing heart to calm, willing her to turn around and walk away. But she stepped closer, slowly but with purpose, all the way up to my oak tree. We were mere feet apart now, and as she rested her one bare hand against the bark of the tree, almost in greeting, the same way I did with all the trees in the wood, I was overcome again.

BRIAR

A GASP SHOOK FREE FROM MY LIPS AS I SUDDENLY beheld a man, just feet away from me on the other side of the tree. His eyes were wild, panicked, and the most perfect shade of mossy green I'd ever seen. He didn't look much older than me, and it took me a second to shake myself out of the daze I'd slipped into admiring his handsome features. My chest told me this was the shadow I'd seen in the trees by the town square, my heartbeat accelerating in the same way it had last night. Not with fear, but with awareness and anticipation. We both stood frozen, staring at one another for a beat too long before I presented my gloved hand holding the necklace out to him.

"Is this yours?" I asked quietly, not wanting to spook him, almost feeling as though I'd happened upon a timid wild animal rather than a well-built man standing over six feet tall. His eyes darted between the necklace in my hand and my face, back and forth and back and forth, until he reached out and gently plucked it from my palm without saying a word. "What's your name?" I tried, offering him a gentle smile. His eyes flashed to my lips for a second, then he cleared his throat and took a step back.

"Theodore," he answered, in a voice that felt like the first bite of a rich chocolate cake. Deep, decadent, and delicious. I felt my cheeks flush in reaction, and I dropped my eyes to my boots. "And what's..." he started, before clearing his throat nervously and my eyes flickered up curiously, eager to hear him speak again. "What's your name?" he said, leaning forward in a way that seemed subconscious, eager to hear my response.

"I'm Briar," I supplied with another gentle smile, and offered my ungloved hand for him to shake. His breath skittered out of him, and he contemplated for a moment before reaching out and taking my hand gently in his.

Electricity jolted from my fingertips all the way up past my elbow as our skin connected, and my eyes clashed with his, as wild and confused as my own. Neither of us dropped the other's hand. We stayed suspended in that moment, eyes and hands locked together for what felt like an age but could not have been longer than a few seconds as fresh snow began to fall around us. I broke eye contact with Theodore first, to watch as a snowflake drifted down and landed on his jumper sleeve before melting away as he finally dropped my hand.

"Briar," he said. Not a question, not addressing me at all, really. I nodded in confirmation anyway, enjoying the way my name sounded on his lips. And when I lifted my head to meet his eyes again, he was gone.

THEODORE

IT HAD BEEN YEARS SINCE ANYONE HAD LOOKED me in my eyes. Acknowledged me, known that I was there. And knowing her name in turn had almost floored me. Briar. Of course. *Briar.* Beautiful, wild, dangerous... inviting.

BRIAR

BY THE TIME I WALKED THROUGH THE FRONT door of the cottage, my basket full of fragrant cedar and pine trimmings, I was soaked through by snow, stiff with cold, and feeling deflated. Mabel and Elsie sat at the kitchen table, stringing dried orange slices onto long pieces of thread by the light of a cluster of candles, and the house was full of that gorgeous citrus smell, making my mouth water. I stuck a warm smile on my face as I entered and plopped the basket down on the table.

"Briar!" Mabel scolded, standing from the table. "You're absolutely soaked through; you'll catch your death." She fussed with my cloak, pulling it off of me and hanging it by the flickering hearth. "Straight into a hot bath for you, miss!" she said, steering me towards the tub as Elsie rolled her eyes and laughed.

Mabel had always been this way, making sure I was taken care of, that I never felt too much like the classic middle child. She parented me herself whenever she felt I needed it, and I'd do absolutely anything for her in return. She was my rock.

I thought about telling her what had occurred in the woods as I soaked my aching joints in the warm water, but this... Theodore... It was just for me.

I didn't want her to worry for me, and I certainly didn't want her to keep a closer eye on me. I enjoyed my alone time, reading beneath a tree or foraging in the woods. I'd hate to have a babysitter whenever I left the house. Mabel enjoyed her alone time, too, and I wouldn't rob her of that. So, I kept my mouth shut and started silently planning my trip back into the woods tomorrow.

I couldn't let this go. I hadn't imagined anything, and I needed answers. All my life I'd believed in magic in some form or another. When I was little, I'd believed in fairies, goblins, and magical far-off lands. As I grew older, my belief never lessened, just evolved. I now believed in the magic of the earth itself. The sun and the moon and the tides, the blooming flowers, the healing herbs, there was so much magic in what most would call the mundane. But this encounter had me questioning everything again. I couldn't explain how the pendant had made me see what I'd seen. I couldn't explain how Theodore had disappeared before my eyes. How much of the stories we read in fairytale books, how much of the myths and legends we heard over campfires in the summer, passed down through generations, was true? I had to learn more.

I started planting the seeds for tomorrow's plan as I sat with my sisters at the table, my damp hair doing its best to dry by the warmth of the fire. We were weaving the greenery I'd brought home today into a wreath for the door, having already made garlands and a centrepiece for the table. "We need some pinecones and holly berries," I declared. "It's too plain. I should have picked some up today." My sisters stepped back and assessed the wreath but before they could tell me it looked fine, or not to worry, I said, "I'll go out and collect some tomorrow." I caught Mabel's disapproving eye and quickly added, "I already know where to go, I'll be much quicker than I was today." That seemed to placate her, and she held her tongue. By the end of the evening, the cottage looked and smelled beautiful. Fresh greenery lay over the mantle and windowsills, citrus garlands hung over the fireplace and in front of the windows, positioned perfectly to catch tomorrow's morning light. We all sipped cups of hot chocolate by the light of the dying embers in the fire and listened to Elsie read one of her favourite winter solstice tales aloud before we all shuffled off to bed.

THEODORE

I'D BROKEN OUR MOST ABSOLUTE RULE IN A heartbeat, just to know her name.

As I walked through the forest in the moonlight, feeling the brush of her skin still lingering on my hand like a phantom, I hoped our meeting was brief enough to fly under the radar of the elders and their guard. That way I wouldn't have to explain what had come over me or *how* she'd seen me, since I had no idea myself.

I vowed to keep my distance from now on.

I needed to do my job and keep out of her way. No more following her around, no more daydreaming about her, no more watching her through the brush in the woods as she foraged. I didn't know what protocol the elders would follow if they found out what had happened, I'd never heard of anyone breaking the rules before. Would I be taken from these lands and assigned a new wilds to tend? Or be thrown into a prison?

I couldn't bear either option. Couldn't bear to be taken away from her.

I needed to know we roamed the same land. To know that her bare feet walked softly over the clovers *I* grew, that she drank cordial made from the elderflowers *I* tended to. Knowing I was the reason that sweetness bloomed on her tongue and stuck to her lips every June... I could live forever like this, I decided. Just knowing I was sustaining her.

Something wild inside of me enjoyed knowing that while I might hold myself back from reaching out and touching her with my own hands, the snow could kiss her eyes, the wind could run its fingers through her hair, and the bite of my cold could will her blood to the surface of her pale cheeks. My magic could touch her, even if I couldn't. And that would have to be enough.

BRIAR

For the second time in as many days, I stepped into the tree line before dawn. The snow had stopped falling and it was even colder today. My boots crunched loudly through the snow that blanketed the fields and the forest floor as I made my way back to the oak tree, uncertain of what I may or may not discover, but determined, nonetheless. Though our meeting had been brief, Theodore didn't feel unfamiliar to me. He felt *right*.

I stopped along my journey to collect pinecones, only taking those that had opened and dropped their seeds already, and I found an abundance of red berry bushes to forage from. I hadn't been lying, the wreaths and garlands *would* look better with these additions.

I took a break when I arrived at the old oak, placing my basket down on a snowy log, and pouring myself a hot tea from the flask Mabel had insisted I bring with me today.

As I took my second sip, the ginger and clove rooibos warming my blood, I heard footsteps coming through the snow and I startled. I slowly set down my cup in the snow, steam billowing into the frigid air, and as I straightened, my eyes fell on two figures in the tree line ahead of me. They were tall and cloaked, and immediately I knew neither one of them was Theodore. There was no feeling of rightness, no tentative curiosity awakening in me, instead my heart bleated with panic.

They moved so gracefully it looked as though they

floated over the snow. I would have believed they were if not for the footsteps I could hear. As they got closer, I could pick out features—one female, one male. They looked almost human, devastatingly beautiful, but something was *wrong* about them. In what felt like no time at all they were mere feet from me, and I was glued to the spot, fear anchoring me. No fight, no flight, just freeze. I gasped as they took down the hoods of their cloaks, revealing two little horns protruding from their temples. Almost like that of a muntjac deer.

"Briar, is it?" The man on the right asked, and all I could manage was a shaky nod of my head. "Such a pretty thing," he murmured before taking a step closer. "Such a shame."

My instincts were screaming at me to run, and I matched him by taking a step back at the same time, keeping the distance between us. He made to step again, when the woman beside him placed a hand on his wrist, halting him. "How is it she sees us, Aleks? Something is unusual here," she said into his ear in a hushed whisper.

"That is not for us to investigate. We were sent with a job to do, not to ask questions." He pulled his wrist free from her grip, and closed the distance between us in a movement so fast my eyes couldn't track it. "I am sorry, sweet Briar. For what I must do next," he said, but before he could move again, I opened my mouth and let a feral scream rip from the very core of me.

I was far from the village, far from houses, my only hope was someone else in the forest hearing and coming to my aid before I found out exactly *what* he must do next. I saw my window of opportunity when he started at the war cry that came out of me, and I dropped to the ground and rolled away, before springing to my feet and sprinting for the tree line, clumps of snow flying everywhere, clinging to my hair, and sliding down the back of my neck.

As I rounded a beech tree, I ran headlong into a knit clad chest that had been running with just as much vigour in my direction. I saw his moss green eyes widen in alarm as we crumpled to the ground. Before I could even try to find my feet, I was being pulled up again and swung behind Theodore, as he put himself between me and the strange horned folk that had come for me. We were both panting heavily as they approached us, my rescuer standing defensively in front of me while I clung to the fabric at his back, peeking around under his arm to see the tall figures stop just metres in front of us.

THEODORE

My mind was racing and I couldn't think straight as my sweet, wild thing clung to my back, closer than we'd ever been before. I told myself I'd stay away, and I meant it, but when I heard that scream rip through the forest, I was already halfway to her before I'd even made the conscious decision to move. To hell with my own consequences, I'd take whatever the punishment was to protect her. But now, standing facing two members of the elder's guard, I realised what punishment they had been sent to carry out. Not to take me away or imprison me—to get rid of her.

"Ah, Theo." Aleks started, shaking his head. "See what you've done? The elders have been watching you closely, they know what you've been doing, but they hoped you'd never cross that line."

"It was one mistake. It won't happen again." I gritted out. Aleks was one of the few guards I'd had the misfortune of training with in my teen years. There was something rotten about him. The woman beside him stepped forward slowly with her hands up. I didn't know her, but she at least looked somewhat apologetic for the situation we were in.

"The thing is, she's seen you now. She knows."

I shook my head, unwilling to accept the words.

"She can't know, Theo," she finished gently, and I knew what she was telling me. This wasn't just a punishment; this was the law. They were sent here to dispatch of her.

Briar seemed to put the pieces together at the same time I did, and I felt her pull away, ready to run again, so I spun and urged her onwards. We stumbled through the snow, ducking under branches and leaping over logs, my hand never leaving her elbow, keeping her upright, keeping her steady.

"Don't make this more difficult than it needs to be, Theodore!" Aleks boomed from much too close behind us before I felt an arm band around my midsection, yanking me backwards. Briar stumbled, and the woman was suddenly there, hauling her up and holding her by the shoulders as Aleks held me back.

"Don't make this worse," he said, gruff in my ear, struggling to keep his grip on me.

The woman pulled a dagger from her cloak, hands shaking, and positioned it at sweet Briar's throat. A roar ripped out of me as I threw my head back into Aleks' face, freeing myself and surging forward. The horned woman dropped Briar as I ripped the blade away and spun to face Aleks.

I launched the dagger at him, too swift for him to deflect. I didn't linger to see if he'd go down, just gripped

Briar's hand and urged her on through the dense, snowy trees.

Briar was panting, and slowing, her human body not able to keep up with my pace. My gaze darted around, looking for salvation and spotting what I was hunting for. I tucked her under my arm and squeezed us into the hollow centre of an old, long-dead tree, the sky open over our heads but partially obscured by some large slate rocks that had rested here for millennia. There was no room to move, her back flush with the farthest wall of the hollow, my back flush with the small opening, and our fronts pressed together much closer than would be deemed appropriate in proper human society. My hand was over her mouth, doing my best to muffle the sound of her loud, shaking breaths while her hot tears splashed onto the back of my hand.

"We shouldn't be found here," I whispered. "As long as we're quiet." It had taken me over a year of roaming these lands before *I'd* even found this spot. When her breathing finally calmed, coming deeper and easier, I removed my hand from her mouth.

"What is happening? Who are they? Who are *you*?" she asked in a barely audible whisper, her limbs shaking either from fright or cold, I couldn't be sure. How could I explain this? She deserved answers, her life was in danger and it was all my fault. She'd seen me disappear in front of her eyes and now she'd seen members of the guard, and while I could pass for human, they definitely couldn't.

"I'm—" I faltered, what could I say? I'm what? An elemental being that gives power to the land she lives on? I'm not human? That all the magic she assumes is in the natural world, but won't admit out loud to believing in, is real?

There she was, standing before me, looking up at me

expectantly with those stunning chalcedony eyes, sparkling and curious. Where should I begin? How much should I divulge?

"I'm not like you," I settled on and her dark brows furrowed together in confusion, but she waited in silence for me to continue. Snowflakes started gathering in her dark waves, on her long lashes, and her cheeks flushed a rosy pink. That thing inside my chest woke up again, delighting in the sight of my power all over her. She tilted her head to the side, and I worried that she'd somehow read my thoughts, before realising it's because I was standing there in silence, taking in her snow-dusted beauty when I should be explaining.

"Do you believe in magic, Briar?" I whispered in the dim light of the hollow, and she shivered in response.

"That depends..." she answered shakily.

"Do you believe in the magic of the natural world? The souls in the trees, the healing power of the sweet rosehips from the flower that gave you your beautiful name?"

She looked taken aback but answered quickly. "Yes." Simple and sure. It was as I'd known. You didn't walk through the trees the way she did without believing.

"Then you believe in me," I told her, and watched her face as she tried to understand.

"You're... magic? Or nature?" she asked, looking for clarification.

"Yes," I said, hoping that would be enough. Her breathing started to get heavy again, but I couldn't cover her mouth. She had to be able to speak, to ask.

"What about the pendant?"

I was trying to take in her questions, but she was standing so close to me I could smell the cinnamon-mandarin scent of her, at odds with her name but at home in the art that was her face and the wildness of her spirit. Her head tilted way back to take me in, standing a good foot taller than her, and the way the winter light shone down into her eyes took my breath away. As I watched her pupils dilate, I forgot anything she'd asked me.

"Briar," I whispered in warning.

"Theodore," she responded, the first time she'd said my name, and I almost fell to my knees right there.

BRIAR

HE LET OUT A LONG BREATH, THE WARMTH tickling my cheeks.

"I made this pendant," he started, his words tentative, as if he was unsure he should be speaking them, "four springs ago."

My mind instantly flew back to the last time I had ventured out here to the river with my sisters. It was a balmy day in May, and I'd hiked up my skirts to wade into the water. We'd stayed out there for hours, laughing and splashing or lying on the bank talking and drinking lemonade we'd brought from home. I'd had that odd feeling of being watched for the very first time that day.

"I... I saw you in the river," he said quietly, already shaking his head as if he shouldn't have divulged that to me. And my pulse started to race. "You were so free, so beautiful, so unlike everything I'd been told humans were. I wanted to know you," he blurted out and I was taken aback.

I was the plainest of my sisters. Elsie and Mabel were so *bright* they glowed in the sunlight, whereas I swallowed it up with my dark hair, my dark clothes and my pale skin that never tanned even after days in the sun.

"Why didn't you say anything?" I asked, disbelieving. His eyes scanned my face, as if looking for the answer there, or deciding what he should or shouldn't say.

"We're not supposed to engage with humans," he admitted quietly, still looking down at me, our clouds of warm breath mingling in the winter air, and I think my heart stopped for a moment entirely. "That's why those guards were sent by my elders. Because I broke the rules." He took a deep breath before continuing "The first time I saw you, I was so overcome, I tried to push the forbidden feelings out of me...They formed the stone and I've worn the pendant every day since."

"Overcome?" I repeated, ignoring my original want for knowledge about the pendant, desperate to hear what beautiful words would spill from his mouth next.

"Utterly overcome, Briar," he answered, voice growing husky. "The only time I've felt human feelings is in your presence. The only time my heart beats is when I gaze upon your face. The only time my blood runs hot is when I watch your body carry you through my forest. When you press this land's fruit to your lips..." He continued, grazing his thumb over my full bottom lip, causing a shallow breath to skitter out of me. "Utterly overcome," he said again, trailing his fingers down the side of my throat before letting his hand fall back to his side.

I'd never been looked at like this, *revered* like this, spoken about or touched like this in my twenty-two years. My body hadn't ever responded to anyone with such need, or felt so *seen*. Theodore wrapped his hand gently around the back of my neck, fingers curling into my hair.

"Stop me, Briar," he whispered into my ear, pressing our bodies together.

"I don't want to stop you," I said, pressing closer against his warm body, making him groan, and finally he brought his mouth down to meet mine. His lips were soft and warm and he tasted like winter peppermint as he completely commandeered my mouth.

My first impression had been wrong, this man was not timid. No, he had simply been *restrained*, and now those restraints had been cut loose, something wild in him calling to something wild in me. I felt the crumbling bark of the tree hollow against my back then, all too quickly, he pulled away, panting.

"I'm sorry," he said, running his hands through his hair and pressing himself back against the opening to our hiding spot while I tried to catch my breath. A man restrained once again.

THEODORE

I HAD TO GET OUT OF THAT HOLLOW, HAD TO GET her home safe and away from me. I was a man undone around her, and it was dangerous for us both. We were still hiding from the consequences of our last meeting, and already I was crossing entirely new boundaries. I could not control myself when she was near.

"I need to get you home," I said, straining my ears and trying to survey the space around the hollow, determining the safety of our exit. I hadn't heard the guards come this way, and hopefully by now they had given up, travelling back to report to the elders and get a healer for Aleks... if he survived.

"Home?" she whispered, surprised. "Won't that be the first place they look? My sisters—" Her hushed words were coming out quickly, full of panic.

"They will not enter your home," I told her, attempting to soothe her panic. "If they did, they'd be breaking the same rule that I have." She didn't look convinced, so I carried on. "We are not to interfere with humans. Out here, in the wilds, they can pursue you. Especially since I've already revealed myself to you—though I don't know how. But in your homes and towns? They cannot and will not set foot there."

She finally nodded, convinced, and I wasted no time in pulling her back under my arm and squeezing us out of our hiding spot, back into the frigid air of my winter forest. She stayed nestled under my arm, though there was no need for us to remain so close now that we had space out in the open again. But I couldn't have pried my arm away if I wanted to.

If these were the last moments I had with her, I'd hold her close.

We moved slowly, ears straining to hear movement and eyes sweeping our surroundings, but all seemed quiet. We collected her things she'd discarded by the oak tree and the closer we got to her home, the more she relaxed into my side.

"You said you don't know how you revealed yourself to me," she started, breaking the silence as we exited the tree line and started across the snowy fields. "That woman had said something similar, too. As if it was unusual. But you were standing right in front of me?"

I felt her lift her chin to gaze up at me as we strode on, trusting me completely to guide her, not needing to look ahead herself. "The average human *can't* see us," I explained, glancing down at her where she looked up at me with big sparkling eyes, waiting for me to go on. "I've walked past many a person in those woods, sweet Briar, and no one has ever seen me. I've all but ran headlong into people, and still they were none the wiser that I was there, mere feet from them. We're supposed to be invisible to you all, nothing more than energy, a feeling, a breeze."

She looked down at her feet again thoughtfully. "Then why can I see you?"

"Because you're special," I said, halting us to hold her by the chin and guide those beautiful eyes back to mine. "I don't know how, or why, but it makes sense to me that you can." We'd be at her cottage soon, and I wasn't prepared to say goodbye to her yet. "We're taught from a very young age all about humans, that they're nasty, greedy, selfish things. This is why we're not allowed to reveal ourselves or intermingle. We're taught that they're the reason we must be assigned wilds to tend to, to help prolong the life of this earth, to balance out the human's destruction."

She looked up at me sadly, but unoffended. Like she believed this to be true, too.

"But I've watched you for years, sweet, wild thing. And there could be nothing purer wandering through my forest. No newborn fawn or rabbit in a burrow more at home with their feet on the earth than you."

Her eyes started to glitter with tears, welling but not yet falling. "What happens now?" she whispered.

"I don't know."

BRIAR

HE TUCKED ME BACK UNDER HIS ARM AND A TEAR turned cold in the icy air as it rolled down my cheek. I'd only just found him, and already we were being separated. The idea of being away from him felt *wrong*, all the way down to my bones. The sun was already setting as we approached the cottage. The windows were lit up with an orange glow from candles and the fire, smoke puffed out of our chimney, and I could hear my sisters singing faintly from within. It looked warm, safe, and inviting, but I didn't want to leave the canopy of Theodore's arm. He stopped at the back gate, far enough that no one inside would spot him, but close enough that I wouldn't be left alone outside of my property line.

"Stay inside," he told me, turning and taking my cold face between his warm hands.

"If you must go out, don't go alone. And stay out of the woods." His own eyes were glistening now.

I nodded, words failing me. Then he bent forward and placed a tender kiss on my forehead. I closed my eyes, breathing him in, and when I opened them, he was gone.

I hardly slept a wink all night. Knowing Theodore was still out there, knowing there would be consequences still set to fall on our heads. I'd spent a good portion of the evening sitting up by my window, gazing out across the fields to the woods beyond, worrying about every possibility.

By the time the sun rose, I was feeling completely numb. I met Mabel in the kitchen, hooking our kettle over the fire.

"Tea?" she offered, and I nodded gratefully. She pottered about making our drinks in a comfortable silence as I took a seat in an armchair by the hearth. "Elsie's gone off into town." She passed me my little mug with fir trees on it and I took an eager sip, burning my tongue. "She said she had a few last-minute gifts to pick up." She let out a sigh as she sank into the other armchair, her auburn hair messy from sleep, glinting in the firelight like an ember. "What's wrong, Briar?" she asked me gently, and when my eyes met hers, I couldn't stop the tears that welled.

She placed her mug on the side table and swiftly came to join me on my armchair, bundling me up in her arms. "You can tell me anything, you know that." Her hands tenderly brushed my messy hair off of my forehead and away from my eyes.

"But it doesn't make any sense!" I sniffled. "You'll think I'm mad," I said, a bit quieter, and glanced up to meet her eyes again. Her face was full of gentle resolve, and she brushed away my tears.

"You are my sister, and I could never think you mad. You could tell me you'd seen a flying pig and I'd rush to look out of the window."

I chuckled at that, as had been her intention, and felt some of the stress start to ease off of my shoulders. I took another sip of my ginger tea, breathed in deeply, and began to recount the past few days to her.

THEODORE

I heard Briar's soft chuckle coming from somewhere in the house as I sat folded into the snowy hedgerow bordering the field behind her cottage. It didn't feel safe to return to the forest. Here, I could hopefully avoid the Elders and be close enough to protect Briar if she needed me.

As I sat in the snow-muffled silence, only occasionally broken by the sparrows flitting in and out of the branches, resting on my shoulders and warming their little feet, I pondered what life would look like now. The order from the Elders was not going to go away, no matter how long I hid here and avoided it. I'd have to go back to the forest eventually. Briar couldn't stay locked up in her house for the rest of her life, either. No human could, least of all her. She needed to feel the ground beneath her feet, trail her gentle fingers through the meadowsweet that grew by the river. She needed to connect with the wilds as much as I did.

Lost in my thoughts, brushing the back of a finger over a robin's soft wings, I didn't see her until she was already halfway across the field.

Briar. Running into the forest.

I launched myself out of the brush, the birds taking for the skies in a cloud around me. I'd lost sight of her as she was swallowed by the snow-heavy trees, but I let my instinct guide me and tracked her as though she was just another creature in my forest. We were just two wild things running through the snow.

I caught a glimpse of her dark hair ahead of me, decorated with fresh snow from the tree boughs she ducked under and brushed against. A few more steps and I could make out her cloak, the charcoal wool almost blending in with the bark of the ash trees around us. And then I was upon her. I pushed myself faster at the same time she heard me and slowed, and we collided in the snow.

We rolled over the cold forest floor, locked together before we came to a stop. Briar panted beneath me, terrified for a second until she realised it was me, and her face relaxed. Her cheeks were flushed red from the run, and her chest was heaving beneath nothing more than nightclothes. She hadn't even gotten properly dressed before she left the house. Her white chemise was much too delicate to keep her warm, even with her cloak around her shoulders, and it revealed more of her than I'd ever seen before. It took me a second to adjust my focus and form words.

"What on earth are you doing, Briar?" I asked, but still didn't move from where I held myself over her.

"The pendant—" she panted. "Where is it? You weren't wearing it yesterday when you took me home." The pendant? My hand instinctively went to my chest, feeling for the silver and the stone, but it wasn't there. I sat up. "It must have come off yesterday in the scuffle," I said, trying to mentally map where we'd been when I was last aware of it hanging around my neck. "How does this explain you running off into the forest when you know the danger that could be out here waiting for you?" I offered her a hand and pulled her up to standing. "We have to get you home right now." I turned us back to face the direction we'd run from, but she pulled her hand from mine and stayed rooted to the spot.

"We have to get it back, Theodore!"

"It's not important!" My panic and concern over her safety prevented me from assessing how that might sound, and caused my voice to rise more than I'd intended. She looked at me as though I'd slapped her. Her chin wobbled and she turned her face away from me.

"Well, I'd like to get it back. It's important to me, even if it's not to you."

"No, no, sweet thing," I murmured, taking her hands in mine. "Of *course* it's important to me. But it's not more important than your *life*." I placed gentle kisses on her knuckles, but she pulled her hands away.

"I'm going to find it, Theodore, with or without you." Her face was set, her eyes determined. I couldn't very well throw her over my shoulder and run her home, as much as I'd like to, and the longer we stayed out here arguing, the longer she was in danger.

So, I let out a sigh. "Okay." I pulled my wool jumper off over my head and handed it to her to put on under her cloak. "But *quickly* Briar."

Her face broke into a triumphant and wicked smile as she took my jumper from me and shrugged off her cloak and, for a second, she looked like a mischievous fox standing there in the snow.

BRIAR

WE RUSHED THROUGH THE WOODS, OUR HANDS clasped together, in the direction of yesterday's hideaway. I'd only told Mabel half of the story before it had suddenly dawned on me that I hadn't seen the pendant around Theodore's neck when he'd walked me home.

It was too special to be lost to time, and I didn't know if the elders he'd mentioned would come after him next if they found this stone, full of forbidden human feelings. All self-preservation flew out of the window at the thought of Theodore being the next target of their wrath.

I'd told Mabel I'd finish explaining later, then I grabbed my cloak and boots and ran right out of the back door before she could stop me. The run had warmed me some, but I was definitely cosy now in Theodore's wool jumper. It smelled like roasting chestnuts and fresh fir and *magic*, and I subtly inhaled the scent whenever he wasn't looking. He was down to just a soft, long-sleeved top now, but the cold didn't seem to be affecting him.

He slowed as we neared the site of the oak tree where this had all begun, and after listening for a moment and deeming it safe, we crept into the clearing. As we circled the tree, eyes scanning for the pendant, a keen awareness creeped over me.

"Theo—" I started, but before I could even finish saying his name, I was grabbed from behind and hauled back. Theodore's head snapped up, but he didn't fight or yell like he had yesterday, he froze. I was passed behind my captor, into other arms, until I was standing behind two large, cloaked figures, and held by a third. I watched Theodore through the gaps between their shoulders, and his eyes found mine. Then something glinting on the ground pulled my attention away. The pendant. Half-buried by snow, directly between us. Theodore's eyes followed mine, then darted between my captors and the stone, back and forth, back and forth. I could tell he was trying to gauge if he could grab it before they spotted it, but as he lunged, so did they.

He was too slow. I could only see the backs of the cloaked figures ahead of me as the largest one spoke, holding the pendant up in front of his face by the chain.

"What's this?" he asked Theodore, in a voice so still and cold, goosebumps raised on my skin.

"I don't know." Theodore shrugged. "A necklace? One of the village folk must have dropped it. It's litter, really, so I was just going to..." He was trying his best to seem nonchalant, but even I could see his pulse quickening in his neck.

"Just a necklace?" The other cloaked figure asked in a softer voice than the first, before reaching her hand out to take it from her partner.

"Then why—" Her fingers touched the stone within

the silver and her words cut off as she dropped to her knees. The hands that held me around my upper arms slacked for a moment, as if their instinct had been to rush to her aid before remembering they had to keep a hold of me.

"Vivienne?" The large man turned and crouched down, looking into the woman's unseeing eyes, revealing his profile to me. He was handsome, like Theodore, but like the guards yesterday, there was something *off* about the beauty. Where Theodore looked like nature personified, windswept and snowkissed, these people looked anything but natural. "Vivienne!" he said again, shaking her gently by the shoulders while we all stood and watched, rooted to the spot, unsure what was happening or what to do. Finally, he looked down at the stone still between her fingers and made to yank it free of her grasp. Only, when he touched it, he entered the same unseeing state.

The person behind me shifted, now outnumbered and unsure, and I took my chance to shake free from their hold and rush into Theodore's arms. When I looked back, I saw it was the same woman from yesterday that had held me, assessing us and the cloaked figures on the ground, wary and confused.

"I don't know what's happening," Theodore whispered to me, not taking his eyes off of the two kneeling in the snow.

"I think I do," I said softly. They were unharmed, still here, but I knew they weren't seeing snow right now. Knew they must be smelling hawthorn and watching green leaves dance in the breeze. "This is how I found you." And I told him about the night I found the pendant, what it had shown me, what I had done after.

The guard still standing let out a gentle gasp. "Theo, you made a soul stone?".

"A what?" We answered in unison, but she didn't answer us. She walked closer to the kneeling figures in the snow, inspecting them.

"How did you get out of this?" she directed at me.

"I just took my fingers off of the stone. I was still aware of my body, even when my mind was transported elsewhere." I didn't know why they had stayed this way so long. If we should leave them and make a run for it, or break them free of the stone. I didn't get to make that choice, as the guard reached out to pry their fingers from the pendant.

THEODORE

As their hands came free of the stone and I watched their eyes focus again, I pulled Briar behind me, unsure of what any of this meant, what would happen now.

"A soul stone," Vivienne said, breaking the silence as we all held our breath.

"Yes," the guard from yesterday breathed. Elder Mikael just looked at us, astonished.

I waited for them to say more, but they just sat there, still processing, looking at us with awe.

In the end it was Briar who broke the quiet.

"What is a soul stone, sir?" she asked Mikael clearly. Ever the wild thing, willing to talk with the unusual or feral. I'd seen her approach all manner of creatures in the forest, from the largest stags to the smallest dormice that would send some other humans jumping up onto chairs. She'd approached me. She was, for the most part, fearless. Mikael and Vivienne stood and faced us, and I braced myself.

"A soul stone," Mikael started, "is so rare, it's not thought of as more than a mere myth to most elementals. I have only heard of one other in all my years as an elder."

"They are the product of nature's truest love," Vivienne continued. "They are only created when nature herself blesses a pairing. Often knowing of a love before it even grows. I've never seen it happen in my lifetime, and never before between an elemental and a *human*."

My heart was racing faster now than it ever had. Briar and I were Blessed by nature herself. Every ache of need I'd ever felt and pushed away, every time I'd had to force myself in the opposite direction so I wouldn't be overcome by her entirely, and all along, nature had blessed it, willed it.

"What does this mean for us, for this?" Briar said, gesturing to us all standing in the clearing and the current situation.

The guard from yesterday spoke before either Elder could.

"Anyone blessed by the laws of nature cannot be harmed. It goes directly against what we were born to do. We couldn't even if we wanted to."

My breath washed out of me in a massive wave of relief.

"I saw the elements of your soul in that stone, Briar," Mikael said. "And I can think of no one more deserving of keeping our secret."

BRIAR

MY HEAD SWAM WITH THE NEW INFORMATION, and I barely registered what was said as Theodore left my side to shake hands with the Elders and the guard who now introduced herself as Fia.

Blessed? Theo and I were blessed by *nature* herself.

Suddenly all the things I couldn't explain made sense. The big feelings I'd had for a man I *should* have regarded as a stranger were no longer questionable, but inevitable. The lengths I'd gone to these past few days were no longer ridiculous, but necessary.

A laugh slowly bubbled up from my lips and drew their attention back to me, all regarding me with a quizzical brow, except for Theo, who just smiled warmly before breaking into a laugh, too.

He crossed the distance back to me and lifted me into his arms, spinning us once in the snow before gently placing me back down onto my feet. A polite cough broke the spell, and we turned to find Mikael, Vivienne and Fia smiling at us.

"We will leave you in peace now, young ones," Vivienne said, holding the stone out by its silver chain for Theo to take. "The story we saw in the stone needs to be written for the elemental's archives, and I like to do it while the feeling is fresh." She winked before all three of them vanished back into the treeline.

I turned my focus back to Theodore to find him already gazing down at me. He brushed the back of a warm finger over my cheekbone and I tilted my face up further, willing him to kiss me again like he did yesterday.

"Sweet Briar," he started, and I smiled. "I think it's time for you to learn some magic."

Don't forget...

Thanks so much for reading! If you
have two seconds, please leave a
rating/review for your fellow readers.
We appreciate every single one!

Want more from these authors? Why
not follow us on social media, or join
our newsletter list for extra goodies
and behind the scenes!

Coming soon

Callie Dahl

When Balance Burns

Thieves of Starlight

Jade Church

Ashvale #2

Midnight Haze

Still Yours

Baby, It's Homicide

The Lingering Dark

Jenna Weatherwax

The Curse of Thunder

Helena V Paris

Shadows in the Deep

Men feared monsters. Yet fear made
men do monstrous things.

A slow burn romantasy with
monsters, gods, and a girl who might
save, or doom, them all

The fates are cruel, but she is crueler...

An enemies to lovers, sapphic
romantasy with exclusive
content from Kobo Originals

Can you truly be whole with only
half your soul?

Steamy poly romance and
Greek mythology meet in this
series of standalones

Will there ever be peace in Atlantis when the gods are involved?

This is the Greek mythology romantasy adventure you've been waiting for...

Weaving worlds within wax,
transporting you with atmospheric
candles hand poured with love.